As soon as his daughter was out of earshot, Carson snagged Phoebe's elbow with a gentle hand.

Warmth spread in tingles up her arm as she turned a questioning gaze to him.

"Listen," he said. "I really appreciate you working with Heidi on this."

Up close, she saw that his brown eyes were flecked with the barest hint of gold. Fighting the urge to stare, she focused her gaze on his nose. "I sense she's a good kid who's had a tough time lately. As I said before, the move had to be hard on her."

"Unfortunately, there's a lot more to it than that. But she's not a bad kid," Carson said.

She met his tawny gaze, and for just a moment, she couldn't look away, could barely even breathe. Her stomach dropped, and her legs trembled. Where in the world had he gotten those unbelievable eyes...?

Books by Lissa Manley

Love Inspired

*Family to the Rescue
*Mistletoe Matchmaker
*Her Small-Town Sheriff

*Moonlight Cove

LISSA MANLEY

decided she wanted to be a published author at the ripe old age of twelve. She read her first romance novel as a teenager when a neighbor gave her a box of old books, and she quickly decided romance was her favorite genre. Although, she still enjoys digging into a good medical thriller.

When her youngest was still in diapers, Lissa needed a break from strollers and runny noses, so she sat down and started crafting a romance, and she has been writing ever since. Nine years later, she sold her first book, fulfilling her childhood dream. She feels blessed to be able to write what she loves, and intends to be writing until her fingers quit working or she runs out of heartwarming stories to tell. She's betting the fingers will go first.

Lissa lives in the beautiful city of Portland, Oregon, with her wonderful husband of twenty-seven years, a grown daughter and college-aged son, and two bossy poodles who rule the house and get away with it. When she's not writing, she enjoys reading, crafting, bargain hunting, cooking and decorating. She loves hearing from her readers and can be reached through her website, www.lissamanley.com, or through Love Inspired Books.

Her Small-Town Sheriff

Lissa Manley

Love Inspired

Recycling programs
for this product may
not exist in your area.

™ LOVE INSPIRED BOOKS

ISBN-13: 978-0-373-81622-4

HER SMALL-TOWN SHERIFF

Copyright © 2012 by Melissa A. Manley

www.LoveInspiredBooks.com

Printed in U.S.A.

Therefore, since we are justified by faith, we have
peace with God through our Lord Jesus Christ.
Through Him we have obtained access
to this grace in which we stand, and we rejoice
in the hope of sharing the Glory of God.
—*Romans* 5:1

For Laura and Sean, who have always encouraged and supported me. I love you.

Chapter One

Sheriff Carson Winters hustled down the boardwalk of Moonlight Cove, his gut clenched, the peace of his day shattered.

What kind of trouble had Heidi landed herself in now?

They'd only been in town a few weeks, and already his daughter had been called into the principal's office for talking back to her science teacher and skipping class.

Despite being grounded for both incidents, Heidi was still definitely acting out, and frankly, he was beyond worried. Being almost thirteen was difficult for almost every kid; add to that the stress Heidi had been through in the past two years and you basically had a single dad's nightmare in the form of one upset, rebellious preteen.

Squinting, he adjusted the brim of his campaign-style sheriff's hat, glad the May rain had stopped for a bit and that the sun was peeking out today. Being from

Seattle, he was used to the Washington state weather, but always had had enough of the drizzle around this time of year.

The woman who'd called him—someone he hadn't met yet named Phoebe Sellers from I Scream for Ice Cream on Main Street—had merely said she needed to talk to him about his daughter. For Heidi's sake, he hoped that whatever she'd done wasn't too serious; the last thing she needed was more difficulties heaped on top of having to deal with her mother's abandonment and her brother's death.

CJ, his boy...

Grief welled up, sharp and searing, taking Carson's breath away. With swift precision he shoved the agonizing memories of his son into their hole.

Instead, he focused on finding the ice cream store. He walked another half block past the planters filled with colorful flowers dotting the boardwalk, then he spotted the small storefront across the street and down a block, sandwiched in between a kite shop and an art gallery.

He headed to the next corner and crossed, then made a left. He looked around as he walked, taking in the quaint storefronts lining the boardwalk and the wooden benches placed here and there for those wanting to leisurely enjoy a treat from the bakery, candy store or ice cream parlor.

As he passed an alleyway separating two buildings, the cool, sea-scented breeze washed over him, carrying the echo of the ocean pounding a block away.

The tight muscles in his neck relaxed a bit, and a bit of his stress eased, confirming that he'd made the right decision by moving here. Moonlight Cove had just the kind of tranquility he'd craved for himself and Heidi since that awful day CJ had died and their world exploded.

As Carson drew near his destination, he tipped his hat to a group of elderly tourist couples wearing matching rain slickers coming out of the art gallery. They greeted him with smiles and respectful nods, and as always, a sense of pride filled him; he was glad he'd followed in his father's footsteps and had gone into law enforcement.

As he opened the brightly painted door of I Scream for Ice Cream and stepped inside, bells rang over his head, announcing his arrival. He immediately smelled the scent of waffle cones and his mouth watered on cue. Guess he should have had more than coffee for breakfast. His appetite just hadn't been the same since CJ died.

The parlor was decorated in shades of green and hot-pink, and had a long counter with swiveling stools along the front wall. The soda-fountain area sat behind the counter, and five or six white tables were arranged in the middle of the place. The wall to the left housed shelves that held bins filled with candy of every kind. A literal dentist's nightmare.

At the moment, the place was empty, which he was grateful for; he'd rather deal with Heidi's trouble without witnesses. Moonlight Cove was their new home, and Heidi needed a clean slate as much as he did.

Just as he hit the middle of the store, a pretty woman with long, curly blond hair stepped out from the back. She stopped in her tracks when she saw him, hesitating for a moment.

She wore a pink shirt with a lime-green apron embroidered with the name of the shop across the front and jeans that showed off her trim yet curvy figure. She looked to be a bit younger than his own age of thirty-two.

"You must be Sheriff Winters," she said, tipping her head slightly to the side.

"Yes. Carson Winters." Moving toward her, he extended his hand. "Guess the uniform gave me away."

She smiled, showing cute dimples on both cheeks, then took his hand. "Yes, the uniform definitely makes an announcement. I'm Phoebe Sellers, the owner, by the way."

He tried to ignore those fascinating dimples. "I figured that. The uniform gives you away, too." He flicked a finger at her pink shirt and lime-green apron. He noted she was tall for a woman—five-eight, at least—and she had clear blue eyes, a smooth, fair complexion and an appealing fan of freckles across her nose.

Very attractive.

She laughed, then moved back a little. "I'm sure you're wondering why I called."

"You would be right." Unfortunately.

Phoebe stepped behind the counter and picked up a cloth, then shoved it into the pocket on her apron.

Observant out of habit, he noticed she wore no wedding ring.

"There's really no way of sugarcoating this…" she said.

Carson nodded curtly, preparing for the worst. "No need to." As a lawman, he was used to handling the ugly truth. Although hearing about his own daughter's trouble…well, not much prepared a father for that.

"Okay," Phoebe said. "The truth is, I caught your daughter shoplifting earlier today."

His stomach pitched. *Theft.* "Oh, no." No small thing; technically, Phoebe could press charges against Heidi, and things would go downhill from there, fast.

He looked up at the ceiling and dragged in a huge breath, then settled his steady gaze on Phoebe. "What happened?" he asked with deceptive calm, knowing that Heidi had ditched Mrs. Philpot.

"She came in with a few friends and hung around over there by the candy. I thought I spotted her swipe something, so when they left without paying or ordering, I politely asked her to show me the contents of her coat pocket." Phoebe nodded to a pile of candy on the counter. "That's the contraband over there."

He looked to where she'd pointed. Saltwater taffy. Heidi didn't even like the stuff. Said it was gross and stuck in her teeth.

Phoebe continued on. "I got her to give me your name and number, and I told her I'd be calling you. I also suggested she might want to head home right away."

"Thank you." He pulled out his cell phone. "Let me call the babysitter and be sure Heidi's back home."

He called and Mrs. Philpot answered. Carson told her what Heidi had done, and an obviously stunned Mrs. Philpot told him, yes, Heidi was there, and, no, she wasn't aware Heidi had left.

Carson breathed a sigh of relief that his daughter was safe and sound, which was tinged by exasperation at what she'd done. Before they hung up, Mrs. Philpot apologized profusely for letting Heidi slip out—and back in—under the radar. Carson eased her mind, telling her that a devious preteen bent on sneaking out could dodge just about anyone.

He said goodbye and disconnected, then turned his attention back to Phoebe, who'd busied herself scooping ice cream for a family of four who'd come in while he'd been on the phone.

"I am so sorry," he said to Phoebe when the customers had left. "Heidi…well, she's been acting out a bit lately, doing dumb stuff."

Phoebe regarded him steadily for a moment. "You guys are new in town, right?"

"Yep. We arrived a few weeks ago."

"Heidi said her friends dared her to steal something, and I got the notion that she was trying to impress them."

"I'm sure she was." He shook his head, his jaw tight. "But that's no excuse for shoplifting, and I've raised her to know the difference between right and wrong."

Carson paused and then forced himself to say, "Do you want to press charges?" He reached into his utility belt and pulled out his pen and notepad. "You have every right to." And that didn't bode well for Heidi. Great.

Phoebe pulled in her chin. "Oh, goodness, no," she said, shaking her head. "That's not why I called you."

Relief wound its way through Carson and his shoulders relaxed a bit. "What would you like to do?"

"I'm willing to cut Heidi some slack because I actually felt a bit sorry for her."

Carson's hackles raised. How much did Phoebe know about him and Heidi, anyway? Had the whole town been talking about their history? How his son had been killed and how Carson's wife had cut out? The thought of being the subject of rampant gossip really rubbed him the wrong way. That's one of the reasons he'd he'd wanted a fresh start in Moonlight Cove.

Despite his thoughts, he managed to give Phoebe the benefit of the doubt. "Because?" he asked in what he hoped was a mildly inquisitive rather than defensive tone.

"It's just I think it must be hard to be the new kid on the block," she explained. "Especially in a small town where a lot of kids have grown up together."

Carson breathed a sigh of relief; it was good to know Phoebe wasn't feeling sorry for Heidi because they'd been fodder for idle town gossip. He also had to admit he was thankful she wasn't going to grill him about what had brought them to town. Talking about CJ's death and Susan's desertion...not happening right now.

He studied Phoebe's pretty blue eyes again, but found no hint of pity. "The move *has* been hard on Heidi," he replied. Especially following on the heels of so many other traumatic events. She'd had to handle more than any twelve-year-old should in her short life. But wrong was wrong. Period. No excuses.

Shifting so that the heavy leather of his belt and holster creaked, he nodded toward the pile of taffy. "While I appreciate your compassion, what she did was wrong, and I insist she pay you back somehow," Carson said.

Phoebe smiled. "It's just candy, and I got it all back. Payment isn't necessary."

Setting his jaw, he said, "I think it is." He looked around. "Maybe she could do some chores around here for the next week or so."

"I don't know..."

"I insist," he said, holding up a hand. "Really. It's not a good idea to let this behavior slide by. She did the crime, she needs to do the time."

Phoebe inclined her head to the side in obvious capitulation. "Okay, then have her come by one day this week after school and I'm sure I can find something for her to do."

"I will. And I'd appreciate it if you could give her some kind of less-than-pleasant chore, like dishes or cleaning bathrooms."

"Spoken like a true parent," Phoebe said, showing those dimples again.

"You've got that right," he replied. Although sometimes, when Heidi rolled her eyes at him, he felt like the most clueless dad alive. "She needs to learn that choices have consequences. She hates any kind of cleaning, so that makes the most sense in my mind."

"Got you."

"And feel free to make her sentence last awhile. I really want her to know she messed up royally." Despite what Heidi had been through, it was important his daughter grow up with boundaries.

"I'll keep that in mind," Phoebe said. "Why don't we say she'll work for me starting this week, and maybe on Saturday, too. All right?"

"Sounds good," Carson said, really liking the way Phoebe had approached the situation. She was obviously a softhearted, sensible woman. "I'll stop by with her after school tomorrow so you two can meet under better circumstances, then she can start on Wednesday." And he'd be sure Heidi apologized. Profusely. After the fact was better than never, in his book.

"Okay. I'll be here all day."

He adjusted his hat. "Thank you for calling me about this."

"You're welcome," she replied with a smile. "I'm not a parent, but if I were, I'd want to know if my kid tried to steal something."

"I do want to know. Being a parent is about the good, the bad and the ugly." Too bad he and Heidi had more than their share of ugly lately.

"Well, it sounds like you're doing all the right things," Phoebe said.

He wasn't so sure; he felt as if he had been thrust into a pitch-black room with no flashlight, only to be told he had to put a complicated puzzle together. Being a single dad was daunting. "Thanks," he said. "And again, thanks for calling me."

Bells over the door jingled, and a customer walked in, interrupting their conversation.

Phoebe looked to the front of the store. "Hey, Molly," she said, waving.

Carson turned and saw a petite redhead heading toward them.

The newcomer waved. "Hey, Phoebs."

As Molly drew closer, her gaze ping-ponged between him and Phoebe. Then Molly's mouth curved into what looked like a sneaky smile. He had to be imagining that devious grin.

"Whatcha doing?"

For Heidi's sake, Carson hoped Phoebe would keep mum about what his daughter had done.

Phoebe narrowed her eyes and stared at Molly for just a second. "I'm talking to Sheriff Winters here." She looked at him. "Have you met Molly Kent yet?"

"Nope, sure haven't."

"Sheriff Winters, Molly Kent," Phoebe said. "Molly owns Bow Wow Boutique down the street."

He shook hands with Molly.

"He stopped by for some ice cream," Phoebe said casually, turning her attention to him. "What'll it be, Sheriff?"

Grateful for Phoebe's discretion, and feeling re-markably hungry now that the waffle-cone smell had done a number on him, he said, "How about a scoop of Rocky Road? It's my favorite."

Phoebe nodded, smacking her lips. "Mine, too. Good choice."

She went behind the counter, grabbed a cone and then started scooping.

"So, you're replacing Sheriff Billings, right?" Molly asked.

"That's right." Gerard Billings, an old friend of Car-son's dad, had been sheriff here in Moonlight Cove for over thirty years and had taken his pension and retired to Arizona just a month ago.

Molly sat on one of the swiveling stools by the coun-ter. "The town was sad to see him go after so long."

"I know. I have some big shoes to fill."

"What made you want to come to Moonlight Cove?" Molly asked.

Thank goodness he had a decent cover story. Just as long as people didn't ask too many *whys*. "My cousin, Lily Rogers, lives here, and I liked the thought of being near family." Although anywhere that wasn't

Seattle probably would have been fine with him. Too many heartbreaking memories there.

"Oh, I hadn't heard you were related to Lily. I know her from the local church's singles' group, which I attended before I got engaged," Molly said. Her gaze made a trip to his ring finger. "Maybe you should go sometime, meet a few other singles…?"

He didn't go to church—hadn't been raised to, actually—and his schedule usually didn't allow him time for many social activities. And a singles' group? Not for him. But he was sure Molly wouldn't be interested in any of that. So instead he said, "Thanks. I'll keep that in mind."

Phoebe interrupted them by handing him his cone. "I made it a double," she said. "You can never get too much Rocky Road."

He widened his eyes. "This cone is huge."

"A big guy needs a big cone," Phoebe said with an impish grin, her pretty blue eyes sparkling.

Male interest shot through him like a bright, undeniable spark, and for just a second, he couldn't take his eyes off her lovely face.

Guess I'm not dead after all….

Iron walls came down around that thought, ruthlessly cutting it off in its tracks. He had no business even being remotely attracted to a woman. Who'd want that kind of turmoil again? Not him.

Cone in hand, he said to Phoebe, "What do I owe you?"

"It's on the house."

"Well, thanks for the ice cream." He turned to Molly. "Nice to meet you."

"You, too," she said, flashing him a bright smile. "Stop by anytime. Phoebe loves visitors."

Phoebe gave Molly an obviously significant glare, then regarded him. "Glad you could stop by, Sheriff."

Was she blushing? And why did he like the look on her so much?

His neck burning, he raised his cone in the air. "Me, too. I'll see you ladies later."

He stepped outside, noting that the clouds had rolled in off the Pacific Ocean again. Rain was sure to follow.

Pausing for a moment, he looked up and down the main street of Moonlight Cove, soaking in the small-town charm and tranquility that had drawn him here. Setting his jaw, he started walking back to the station, one thought foremost in his mind: as long as the town was all he was drawn to, he'd be just fine.

Her cheeks still warm, Phoebe started wiping off the already clean counter. She surreptitiously watched Sheriff Winters go, liking the confident way he carried himself and his decidedly male way of moving. She didn't want to let on to Molly that she found him attractive, though. Oh, no. That would be a disaster.

As the resident matchmaker, Molly would grab ahold of any tidbit of Phoebe's interest and never let go. When it came to getting people together, Molly was tenacious. Especially since she'd found true love recently and was engaged to be married to Grant Roderick next month. As far as Molly was concerned, everyone needed the happiness she'd found with Grant.

Especially Phoebe.

Phoebe was having none of it.

Molly interrupted her thoughts. "Sooo," she said, her voice high, as if she were curious and scheming at the same time. "He seemed nice."

Very nice, indeed. Phoebe kept wiping the counter, carefully moving and putting back the metal napkin dispensers as she went. "Yes, he did."

"Handsome, too." Molly tapped a finger on the counter. "I've always thought dark hair and eyes were a good combination."

Actually, Phoebe found the combination very appealing on the sheriff, too. Not that she'd let Molly know that. "Really? Hmm. I guess so."

"He's tall, too," Molly said. "I like a tall man."

"I suppose." Being tall herself, Phoebe had always preferred bigger guys.

"In good shape I'd say."

Phoebe stopped wiping the counter and frowned at Molly. "How do you know he's in good shape?" She scoffed. "It wasn't like he was dressed in workout gear."

Molly grinned, her blue eyes sparkling. "Let's just say he filled out the uniform just right."

Phoebe's cheeks heated again. Yes, he had made the

uniform look mighty good. What was it about a man in uniform, anyway?

Truthfully, when Phoebe had come out of the back and saw him standing in the middle of her store, she'd actually stopped and stared. Sheriff Winters was easy on the eyes, no doubt about it, all tall, dark and handsome. The blue uniform added interest, of course, but she was pretty sure he'd look good in anything he wore.

"I guess so," Phoebe said offhandedly, throwing the towel in the bin under the counter. "I wasn't really paying attention." Well, maybe a little…

Molly snorted. "Oh, come on, Phoebe. A woman would have to be blind not to notice how good-looking he was."

No kidding. "So he was handsome," Phoebe said, shrugging. "So are half of the guys in this town." Actually, maybe a quarter of the guys around Moonlight Cove. On a good day.

"I didn't notice a wedding ring," Molly said, resting her chin on her fist. "I've heard he's single. Divorced, actually."

Really? Very interesting. A handsome single dad…

With a mental admonition, Phoebe jerked her thoughts back to where they belonged—figuring out how to derail Molly the matchmaking train.

Phoebe held up her hands. "Okay, Moll, let's just cut to the chase." Sometimes direct was the way to go when Molly was on a matchmaker tear.

Molly blinked, the picture of blushing innocence. "About what?"

"Don't try to act like you're not on another one of your matchmaking quests." Phoebe adjusted the straw holder on the counter to its proper position. "I could see your ploy coming from a mile away."

Molly's chin went up. "So what if I am? Can I help it if I want you to find the same happiness I have?"

Reminder time. Again. "I'm not interested in dating." Phoebe hoisted up a brow. "Remember?"

"But—"

"You know this, and you know why." Phoebe drew in a large breath. "I don't want to date anyone ever again." She'd found true love once in Justin, and when he'd died two weeks before their long-awaited wedding...well, sadly, inevitably, so had her hopes for love.

Molly came over, then drew Phoebe into a hug and squeezed her tight. She moved back, her green eyes intent on Phoebe's face. "But what if there's someone else out there for you?"

Phoebe's eyes burned, and she pulled away, then wiped a waffle-cone crumb off one of the stools. "There isn't," she said, covering up the sadness and emptiness her words brought forth with an emphatic tone. "You know I don't believe in second chances."

"I didn't, either, and I found Grant," Molly said.

"I'm not you. Justin was it for me, and I'm okay with that." What other choice did she have? Jump back into another relationship, just waiting for something bad to happen, for her heart to be ripped out of her chest? No, thank you.

Molly opened her mouth to speak. To argue, Phoebe was sure.

She held up a rigid hand again. "No, Molly." She had to be ruthless here or Molly would go into matchmaker overdrive and have double-wedding plans mapped out in no time flat. "I am not interested in dating anyone, so don't try and fix me up with the new sheriff. Besides, he has a kid." She swept the pile of contraband off the counter into a bowl before Molly noticed it. "A preteen." She sighed. "I don't think that's God's plan for me.

"You'd be a great mom," Molly said.

Longing pierced Phoebe's heart, and words stuck in her throat. Sadly, with no chance for a husband, kids weren't in her future. She simply shook her head.

"Well, I think you're making a mistake," Molly said. "Love comes when you expect it the least."

"Love? You're getting a little ahead of yourself here." Phoebe laughed, but it sounded hollow.

Molly's words had a knot forming in Phoebe's chest; oh, how she wished she could convert to Molly's way of thinking. But she couldn't. Justin had been her one true love, and there wouldn't be another. Period.

"No, I'd be making a mistake if I let you fix me up with anyone when I'm sure I'm never going to fall in love again," Phoebe said. "Total waste of time."

"I didn't want to fall in love, either," Molly said. "And I was wrong."

"I'm not wrong about this," Phoebe stated. "So please back off and quit trying to convince me otherwise."

Molly reluctantly agreed, then said goodbye to go back to work.

Phoebe headed toward the freezer to check inventory, and her eyes snagged on the candy under the counter she'd confiscated from Heidi Winters. Unbidden, memories of Carson Winters's dark, chocolate-brown eyes and stunning smile flashed in her brain. He really was a handsome guy.

On top of that, she had to admit she liked the way he'd dealt with his daughter's shenanigans. He seemed levelheaded, fair, and as if he took his parenting responsibilities very seriously.

She'd downplayed her reaction to Carson in order to keep Molly's matchmaking instincts in check. But, truthfully, the new sheriff had piqued Phoebe's interest.

She shook her head. No. Getting caught up in a man—any man—would be heading down a danger-strewn road she was determined to avoid.

Worse yet, Carson made his living in law enforcement, which ranked right up there with firefighter on the dangerous-jobs list in her mind.

She had to remember all of those things, no matter how appealing the new sheriff in town might prove himself to be in the days and weeks to come.

Chapter Two

After work, Carson headed home, dreading the upcoming conversation with Heidi. Given everything else she was dealing with, he hated having to call her on her behavior. But he couldn't let what she'd done slide. Shoplifting was a serious offense, and he had to impress on her that stealing was wrong.

He pulled up to his rented midcentury three-bedroom, two-bath saltbox-style house and parked in the driveway; the garage was still full of moving boxes and extra furniture he hadn't been able to part with when they'd moved. Someday he'd get to sorting through all of it, but right now, just the thought of the chore overwhelmed him and brought forth too many difficult memories.

Turning off the ignition, he sat in his SUV cruiser for a moment, relishing the calm before the inevitable storm. Then he climbed out of his vehicle, locked it and headed toward the front door, figuratively putting his "Dad" hat on.

He let himself in and went directly to the bedroom at the front of the house he used as an office and secured his service weapon in his home lockbox in the closet. He put his sheriff's hat on his oak desk, and then walked through the small, sparsely furnished living room and went looking for Mrs. Philpot.

As expected, she was in the eat-in kitchen standing at the stove making what smelled like Salisbury steak. Carson noted that the chipped tile counters were sparkling clean, and the scuffed hardwood floors looked freshly mopped. Carson didn't require her to do housework, but Mrs. Philpot seemed compelled to keep the place spotless, which he was thankful for. With his schedule, he didn't have much time for housework, and he hadn't had the chance to hire someone to come in and clean.

Today Mrs. Philpot was dressed in a hot-pink tracksuit and white tennis shoes. Her short, bright, unnaturally red hair—colored, he was sure, but, hey, whatever—was, as always, perfectly styled, and her tortoiseshell glasses sat atop her head. Though she was almost seventy, she was as sharp as a tack, and he suspected that today's events were an anomaly; according to her references, not much usually got past her.

Except one determined twelve-year-old bent on misbehaving—his daughter, the escape artist/shoplifter. Wonderful. What a distinction.

"Hello, Mrs. Philpot," he said. "Smells delicious." She usually started dinner so Carson and Heidi didn't end up eating at eight-thirty. That gave Heidi more time to do homework before lights-out at nine. Unless Heidi argued about having to go to bed so early, and then bedtime was more like ten.

"Hello, Sheriff Winters," she said, raising a wooden spoon in the air. "Dinner is almost ready."

"Great." He retrieved a glass from the cupboard and filled it with water.

Mrs. Philpot turned toward him, her hands knotted together, her brow furrowed. "I am so sorry about what happened with Heidi today. She told me she was going upstairs to do her homework, and I was busy vacuuming. She must have slipped out the front door when I was down the hall and couldn't hear or see her." She shook her head. "I heard her music coming from her room, and, silly me, assumed she was still up there."

He put his glass down on the counter. "Please don't worry about this. Apparently Heidi has developed a very sneaky streak, and I'm sure she waited for the opportunity to slip by you and left her music on to throw you off the scent."

"I was just on my way upstairs to check on her when you called…"

"As I said when we talked on the phone, this isn't your fault, Mrs. P. It's Heidi's, and she and I will definitely be talking about her consequence at dinner."

"All right, then. Please let me know how you want me to handle keeping track of her from now on. And remember, Sheriff, this isn't my first rodeo." She winked at him.

Carson blinked, but he was left without an answer; it wasn't as if they could put handcuffs on Heidi.

He walked Mrs. Philpot to the door and she left.

Sighing, Carson stood in the middle of the kitchen, hating that he had to wreck the evening with a lecture.

But there was no help for the serious conversation he and Heidi needed to have.

He called Heidi down to dinner, then went back in the kitchen and got out plates and silverware. Despite the massive ice cream cone he'd eaten earlier today, compliments of the charming Phoebe Sellers, he was starving; he and Heidi would have to talk while they ate.

A few moments later, Heidi called down from upstairs, "I'm not very hungry, Dad."

Classic avoidance.

Sighing, he went to the bottom of the stairs. Heidi sat on the top step, looking mighty worried if you asked him; she was a smart kid, and she knew she'd messed up. She had her long, blond hair pulled back into a ponytail, and she'd changed into gray sweatpants and a white T-shirt as opposed to the jeans or legging thingies she usually wore to school. Her feet were bare, and he noticed she'd painted her toenails a funky blue. Gone were the days she used some demure shade of pink.

"Well, come on down and at least sit with me," he said. "You know I don't like eating alone." Going from a family of four to a family of two almost overnight did that to a guy.

Heidi scrunched up her face. "Do I have to?" she groused.

"Yup, you do." He headed back to the kitchen. "You'll probably get hungry when you see what Mrs. P. whipped up."

Just as he was loading a plate with food, Heidi appeared at the kitchen door.

He motioned her in. "Sure you don't want some?" he asked, holding up the serving spoon. "It looks delicious."

Heidi shrugged. "All right, maybe a little." Guess she was hungry after all if she was willing to step into the fire.

When they were seated at the table, he took a few bites, marveling at Mrs. Philpot's cooking skills. The meal was delicious, and certainly better than the frozen pizza he would have thrown in the oven if she hadn't made dinner.

Heidi sat slumped in her chair and simply pushed her food around with her fork without speaking or looking at him.

He ate and just let the silence sink in for a bit; she needed to stew for while, worry some. When she finally started fidgeting, he cleared his throat and said, "So, as you know, I had a call from Ms. Sellers from the ice cream parlor today."

Heidi studied her plate as if it held the magical key to getting out of the inevitable conversation. After a long silence, she huffed and put her fork down with a clank. "Yeah," she said, her voice defiant. "So?"

His gut burned. "So? You shoplifted, Heidi. What were you thinking?" he asked, his voice low but intense. "Ms. Sellers could have pressed charges."

Heidi slanted a decidedly worried glance at him, biting her lip. "So did she?"

"No, she didn't, luckily for you." He swiped a hand over his eyes, wishing he could wipe away the scene playing out before him. "She could have, though, and probably should have. But she's a nice woman, and she wanted to cut you a break."

"Then what's the problem?" Heidi asked, giving him the classic eye roll.

Dropping his jaw, he stared at her, absolutely flabbergasted. "Are you kidding me? The problem is you snuck out of the house and stole candy."

She said nothing, did nothing. Just sat there, blank. Unrepentant. Who was this sullen kid? What had happened to his little pigtailed daughter with two missing front teeth? The one who actually cared about what he thought? Suddenly he missed that kid, but feared he'd never have her back. Susan leaving had really knocked a hole in their lives, and he'd lost so much more than a wife that stormy winter day Susan had left.

He looked at the ceiling, taking a moment to get ahold of the anxiety bubbling through him. Finally, he said, "Don't you get that what you did was wrong?"

Heidi shrugged. "Yeah, I guess."

Her nonchalance raised his blood pressure another notch. "So why did you do it?"

Nothing.

"Heidi?" he said firmly, resisting the urge to raise his voice. "Tell me."

She let out a huff. "Because Briana and Jessie dared me, okay?"

So Phoebe had been right. Even so, he dipped his chin and just stared at Heidi, as if to say, *you did this on a stupid dare?*

Her eyes glimmered, and he guessed her control was slipping. "They said that I wouldn't have the guts because I was the sheriff's daughter."

Her words hit him like well-aimed bullets, and he winced inwardly. His first instinct was to back off a bit; it probably *was* hard at times to be a small-town sheriff's kid. Kind of like being the minister's kid— expectations were higher somehow.

But, no. He couldn't cave and go easy on Heidi. There was a lot at stake here, and he had to be a strong father for his daughter's sake; a statement about an inch and a mile flitted through his brain. Hopefully she'd thank him someday.

"So you broke the law to prove you weren't chicken," he stated, trying to stay calm.

Suddenly the dam broke, and tears streamed down her cheeks. "Yes, I did," she cried. "They said they'd be my friends if I did it."

Searing pain streaked through his heart, and he resisted the urge to scoop his baby girl into his arms and make everything all right. Poor Heidi. She'd been through so much lately, more, really, than any kid should have to bear. "So you did it to make them like you?" he got out.

Looking at the floor, she nodded.

His throat tightened. What could he say to that? Heidi was the new girl in town, and he knew she desperately wanted to fit in. But, again, he had to be strong, had to keep the big picture in mind. He had to do the hard thing here; parenting wasn't for wimps, and here he was, doing it all alone.

Grim resignation settled down around him.

He fisted his hands, hating what he had to do. "Well, honey, I'm sorry they dangled that in front of you. That was a cruel thing for them to do."

She sobbed, gutting him.

He forced himself to continue. "But you're still responsible for your choices. And you stole, period." He sucked in air, steeling himself. "There has to be a consequence. So Ms. Sellers and I have agreed that you will spend the rest of the week doing chores at her store after school."

Heidi froze, then blinked, clearing her wet eyes. "*What?* Are you kidding me?" Red-faced, she jumped to her feet. "It was no big deal, Dad. Why can't you just let it go? Why do you have to make me work at some dumb ice cream store?"

He tightened his jaw until his head ached. "Because shoplifting was wrong, that's why."

She swiped the tears from her eyes. "You're the

worst dad ever!" she screamed. "Mom wouldn't have made me do this."

More bullets pierced him; Susan was gone and would never make a tough parenting call again. He was on his own.

He let Heidi's comment go, sure she was speaking out of anger, which he couldn't blame her for. He had a boatload of anger, too, mostly directed at himself, though he was also pretty mad at Susan for abandoning them.

Mostly, though, he just felt betrayed.

Heidi turned on her heel and ran out of the room, and he let her go, bleeding inside.

From the hallway she yelled, "And I'm not ever going back to that store and you can't make me!"

Her footsteps clomped quickly up the stairs, and then he heard—and felt—her bedroom door slam.

A sense of failure screamed through him, and he pressed a hand to the bridge of his nose. His appetite gone, he shoved his plate away and slumped back in his chair. With a weary breath he looked around the kitchen, at the old appliances, ugly cabinets and hideous green-and-gold curtains the landlord had probably put up in the seventies.

The place certainly was not a home, nor the peaceful haven he wanted.

A feeling of helplessness spread through him, and suddenly, he'd never felt so alone. He'd lost his son and his wife, and any kind of peace. And now, in a way, he'd lost his little girl, too.

She hated him.

How was he supposed to face that, much less deal with it?

"Sheriff Winters is here to see you."

Phoebe looked up from her desk, trying to ignore the little skip her heart took at the mention of the handsome sheriff. "Okay, thanks. I'll be right out," she said to Tanya, an energetic middle-aged woman who was her lone weekday employee.

"He has a young lady with him," Tanya said, raising her auburn brows. "And she doesn't look very happy to be here."

Not surprising at all. Phoebe was guessing the hammer had come down at the Winterses' last night. "That's his daughter." She rose and stretched the kinks out of her neck. "He said yesterday when he was here they'd be stopping by."

"Why was the sheriff here? Did something happen?"

Phoebe gave herself a mental head slap. Tanya had been taking her daughter to the doctor yesterday when the shoplifting incident had occurred and when the sheriff had stopped by. She wasn't aware of what had happened, and Phoebe wasn't going to fill her in. Heidi's slip-up was nobody else's business.

She waved a hand in the air. "Oh...um...he stopped by for a cone and I told him I'd like to meet his daughter."

Tanya nodded, apparently satisfied with Phoebe's

answer—fabulous—and they both walked out to the main part of the store. Phoebe resisted the ridiculous urge to fluff her hair. Please! Talk about a waste of energy.

Save for Carson and his daughter, the store was thankfully empty. In uniform, he stood, unsmiling, on the other side of the soda-fountain counter, his daughter beside him. He had his big hand on Heidi's shoulder—to keep her from bolting?—and Heidi, dressed in a cute pair of black leggings, boots and a gray coat—was intently studying the floor, her mouth pressed into a decidedly rebellious scowl.

Phoebe felt bad for both of them; this clearly wasn't a fun father/daughter trip to the ice cream parlor for treats.

"Hello, Sheriff," Phoebe said, smiling cheerily to ease the tension, if that were possible. She looked at Heidi. "Hey, Heidi."

Heidi replied with nothing more than a twitch of her mouth.

Carson nodded crisply, all business, his face taut. "Ms. Sellers. Heidi here would like to talk to you."

"Sure." Phoebe cast a surreptitious gaze around and saw Tanya over by the candy shelves, straightening some packages of gummy bears some kids had riffled through earlier.

"Um…why don't we go back to my office," Phoebe said, gesturing to the Winterses to follow her. For Heidi's sake, Phoebe was determined to keep this just between the three of them.

She stepped into her office, pulled two plastic chairs from their spot on the wall and set them before her desk. "Have a seat."

Carson and Heidi sat, and Phoebe moved around behind her desk and settled herself in her desk chair. Folding her arms before her, she looked directly at Heidi, who still hadn't made eye contact. "Thank you for coming by."

Heidi briefly met Phoebe's gaze, then she looked away and shrugged.

Carson's jaw visibly tightened, and his brow furrowed. He took a moment, then removed his hat and set it on his knee, revealing a head of closely shorn thick black wavy hair that would probably be curly if he let it grow. "We didn't come here for your thanks." He paused, probably for effect. "Did we, Heidi?"

"No," Heidi mumbled, shifting on her chair.

Carson let out an impatient sigh, then turned his coffee-hued gaze on his daughter. "What did you want to say to Ms. Sellers?"

Heidi remained silent.

"Heidi?" Carson said in a stern voice. "You need to talk. And cut the *rude* routine."

Heidi seemed to collapse in on herself as her narrow shoulders slumped. Tears formed in the girl's blue eyes, and her face crumbled.

Phoebe's heart went out to Heidi, and she looked at Carson, frowning, trying to tell him nonverbally that she didn't like upsetting his daughter.

Reading her language perfectly, he gave an almost imperceptible shake of his head. No go.

With effort, Phoebe hardened her heart just a bit; she would undoubtedly be helping Heidi more by not cutting her any more slack. Rough for a softie like her, but doable.

Carson focused his attention back on his daughter, who now had tears streaming down her cheeks. His gaze softened, and he reached out and rubbed her upper arm. "Heidi, I know this is hard for you, but you need to speak to Ms. Sellers."

Heidi sobbed, her shoulders shaking, and then looked up, her eyes swimming in tears. "I'm…sorry for…what I did yesterday," she said in a halting voice. "I know it was…wrong, and I won't ever…do it again."

Phoebe's eyes watered and her throat tightened. She looked at the paperwork on her desk, trying to get control. She yanked a tissue out of the box on desk and handed it to Heidi.

Then Phoebe shifted her gaze to Carson. For just a moment, his daughter's agony was reflected in his eyes, and he looked like a concerned dad with mushy guts, one who loved his daughter and hated upsetting her, but knew that a dad had to do what a dad had to do.

Swallowing, Phoebe said, "Thank you for your apology, Heidi, and I accept it. I know coming here wasn't easy, and I appreciate you making the effort."

Heidi finally looked right at her, nodding. "You're welcome."

"I've talked to Heidi," Carson said. "And she's aware that she will be working here after school for the next few days." He turned to Heidi. "Right?"

She heaved out a sigh, defiance making a show. "Do I have to?"

"Yep, you do, honey," he said firmly, but not harshly. "You do the crime, you do the time, remember?"

Heidi pursed her lips. "Dad, you've said that to me about a thousand times."

"And I'll say it a thousand more times if I need to," he replied. Then he cracked a small, wry smile that softened the stress lines tightening his face. "Maybe even a million." He gave Heidi a playful nudge on the shoulder. "You never know."

To Phoebe's relief, his comment seemed to break the ice, and the tension in the room eased a bit more.

And Carson Winters rose a notch in her eyes.

"Daaaaad," Heidi said, wiping at her eyes with the tissue Phoebe had given her. "Don't be so weird."

"Who, me?" he said, his voice brimming with teasing, exaggerated innocence. Then he waggled his eyebrows and made a goofy face. "Are you sayin' I'm a weirdo?"

Heidi's lips curved into an itty-bitty smile. "A big one," she said, rolling her eyes, but in what looked like a playful way.

He gave Phoebe a rueful look, shaking his head. "I'm sure I'm not the first father to be called weird, and I'm sure I won't be the last."

"No, I'm sure you won't," Phoebe replied, glad to see the stress level between father and daughter evening out. At least temporarily. "So," she said to Heidi. "Just come here after school tomorrow, all right?"

Heidi nodded her assent, and then all three of them rose. Phoebe gestured for Heidi to precede her out, and as soon as Heidi was out of earshot, Carson snagged Phoebe's elbow with a gentle hand.

Warmth spread in tingles up her arm as she turned a questioning gaze to him.

"Listen," he said, "I really appreciate you working with Heidi on this."

Up close, she saw that his brown eyes were flecked with the barest hint of gold. Fighting the urge to stare, she focused her gaze on his nose. "I sense she's a good kid who's had a tough time lately. As I said before, the move had to be hard on her."

Nodding, Carson ran a hand through his hair, then put his hat back on. As he did, he said softly, "Unfortunately, there's a lot more to it than that."

Phoebe blinked, so surprised by his unexpected comment she wasn't sure what to say.

At her silence, he continued on, his voice low and taut. "Heidi's mom took off over a year ago, divorced me, and we haven't seen her since."

Her heart knotted. "Oh, wow, I'm so sorry." She touched his arm briefly, trying to offer even a small amount of comfort. Obviously they'd been through the wringer. "That explains a lot."

"Yeah." He shook his head. "I shouldn't have said anything…"

"No, I'm glad you did."

"I guess I just wanted you to know why Heidi is having such a rough time, and why she's acting out. She's not a bad kid."

"Thank you for your honesty, and for the record, I never thought she was a bad kid." She knew it hadn't come easy for him to admit the truth.

"You're welcome," he said, looking right at her.

She met his tawny gaze, and for just a moment, she couldn't look away, could barely even breathe. Her stomach dropped, and her legs trembled. Oh, wow. Where in the world had he gotten those unbelievable eyes…?

"C'mon, Dad. I have homework," Heidi called impatiently, breaking the spell.

Carson looked away, clearing his throat. "Guess I gotta go."

All Phoebe could do was nod.

She followed him out to the front of the store, her cheeks warm. Phoebe stood there for a long moment after they left, unable to forget the tears in Heidi's eyes and the worry lines creasing Carson's face.

Empathy gushed through her.

Granted, she wasn't a parent, and wouldn't presume she could give Carson much advice on that front. But she had been a twelve-year-old girl once. And even though she hadn't been through the heartbreaking childhood trauma Heidi had, Phoebe *had* lost someone she'd loved fairly recently, just as Heidi had essentially lost her mom.

And Phoebe sure knew how much such a devastating loss could tear a person apart and leave them feeling as if nothing would ever be the same again.

As if their world had crumbled into a million pieces.

Maybe she could help them through their troubles in the coming weeks. Talk to Heidi, commiserate a bit. Offer a shoulder to Carson...

Horrified by her thoughts, she closed her eyes and shook her head. No. *Absolutely not.* What was she thinking? Getting too involved with the Winterses would be a huge mistake, and would definitely force her into a personal space she didn't want to be in.

With that thought forefront in her mind, she straightened her shoulders and headed back to her office to return to the paperwork stacking up on her desk.

As she fired up her computer, she promised herself that she would work with Heidi because Carson had asked her to and because presenting a consequence to Heidi was the right thing to do. But after that, Phoebe would be content to say hello to them casually around town once in a while. Nothing more.

No matter how much the tension between father and daughter pulled on her heartstrings and made her want to help chase their worries away.

Chapter Three

Two days after Sheriff Winters and Heidi visited Phoebe's store, she stood in back of the soda fountain, serving George and Lela Raggs.

The bells above the door jingled and a moment later, Molly breezed through with some flowers in one hand. Wedding samples, Phoebe presumed.

Phoebe waved a greeting and Molly gestured back, then hung at the front of the store while Phoebe finished doing business.

Phoebe handed George and Lela their cones. "Let me know how you guys like that new mango ice cream," she said. "Feedback so far has been positive."

"Sure thing, Phoebe," Lela said. "Although you know my favorite will always be Rocky Road." George and Lela, newly retired and loving it, came in every Tuesday and Thursday at precisely two in the afternoon. Today marked the only time in recent memory that Lela had ever ordered anything but a single scoop of Rocky Road. George, on the other hand, was all over the ice cream board, and rarely ordered the same thing twice.

"Lots of people like Rocky Road," Phoebe said. Including the sheriff—but she wasn't thinking about him. "Don't worry. I'll always have that flavor around."

"Excellent," George said. "We'd hate to have to go somewhere else for our ice cream fix."

"I'd hate that, too," Phoebe replied with a smile, even though she was the only dedicated ice cream store in Moonlight Cove proper. "You two are some of my best customers." Sure, lots of tourists frequented her store. But she also had a core group of locals who came in on a regular basis, even when the rain started and the tourist season took a nosedive. Without them, her business would languish in the off-season.

"Say," Lela said, her forehead crinkling. "We didn't see you at church on Sunday. Everything okay? You're usually a regular."

Phoebe picked up an ice cream spade and started smoothing the top of the Rocky Road. "Um…yeah, yeah. Everything's fine. I had to work." True enough. She *had* come in and done the weekly supply ordering.

"Oh. Okay," Lela said. "Hope you'll be able to come next week."

Phoebe smoothed the top of the Rocky Road until it was a literal work of ice cream art, then moved on to the chocolate chip. "I hope so, too," she said truthfully, though she doubted her sentiments would come true.

Since Justin died, she'd dutifully attended church, hoping to bridge the chasm Justin's death had caused between her and God through faithful, regular worship. Yet somehow that strategy hadn't worked, and lately, she'd avoided services, feeling as if her efforts were futile and useless, not to mention frustrating.

A big rut, for sure, one she didn't know how to dig her way out of.

After a bit more small talk about the new restaurant that was rumored to be opening in town, George and Lela said goodbye and headed out into the sunny May afternoon to enjoy their cones as usual—weather permitting—on the benches perched along the edge of the covered boardwalk that lined both sides of Main Street.

Wistfulness rose up in Phoebe; what would it be like to be retirement age and still have the love of your life by your side?

She would never know.

Pushing aside a hollow feeling of loss she didn't want to dwell on, Phoebe wiped her hands, then turned her attention to Molly, determined not to let herself wallow. "Hey, you. What's up?"

Molly held up the flowers in her hand. "What do you think of this color scheme?"

The bouquet held a gorgeous collection of pink, purple and white flowers, interspersed with fluffy greenery and baby's breath.

"I love it," Phoebe said. "Meg really outdid herself." Meg Douglas had recently moved to town to help run the local flower store, Penelope's Posies, with her mom, Penelope Marbury, who was thinking about retirement now that Matchmaker Molly had found her a man. Happily, Penelope and Hugh Jeffers, a local Realtor, were engaged after Molly had set them up six months ago.

"I like it, too," Molly said, eyeing the bouquet from all angles. "And the flowers will go really well with the bridesmaid dresses I've picked out."

Phoebe's lunch gurgled, and the theme to a once popular children's show starring a big purple dinosaur went skipping through her brain. She shifted on her feet and bit her lip, determined not to tell Molly she wasn't terribly keen on the dress Molly had chosen for her attendants.

Okay. So she hated the purple satin number with the puffy sleeves. But she would dutifully wear it for her best friend without complaining because that's what bridal attendants had been doing at weddings since the dawn of time and invention of satin.

"Yes, they will go well with the dresses." She smiled. Big. Like a huge, toothy dinosaur. "The purple especially," she added, even though she feared she was going to look like a shiny grape on the altar. Or maybe an eggplant.

Molly beamed. "Oh, good. I've been really hung up on the flowers."

No kidding. This was the fifth bouquet Phoebe had seen in the past two weeks.

Molly continued on. "Grant says to just pick something, but it's been hard to find just the right combination."

"Well, looks like you've got a winner," Phoebe said, nodding toward the flowers, which were truly gorgeous. Unlike the dress she'd be wearing, which hovered more around fruitlike than gorgeous.

Nodding, Molly set the flowers down. "I hope so, but now that I've picked the flowers, I need to rethink the cake. Any chance you can go to the bakery tonight after work for a tasting?"

"I can't." Phoebe moved the tip jar over an inch so it was in its normal place. "Tonight's the first night of the grief-counseling class I signed up for."

Molly hoisted up a brow. "So you finally gave in to your mom and agreed to go?"

Phoebe let out a breath. "Yeah. I'm not really that hot on the idea, but she really wants me to, and I've never been able to say no to her." She made a face. "Plus, she signed me up, so it's a done deal."

Molly sat on a stool. "Well, I think it's great you're going."

"I don't know. I'm not sure how talking about losing Justin can do any good." Sometimes it felt as if nothing could help soothe her grief.

"You'd rather just ignore the hurt and grief, wouldn't you?" Molly grimaced. "No offense, of course. I don't pull punches."

Phoebe wouldn't expect her to. "I'm not ignoring it," she said, making sure the metal ice cream scoops were arranged in their water bins just so.

"Maybe not totally…"

Phoebe paused. "I'm doing the best I can." But was her best good enough? And without God to help her… well, she *was* struggling, and she wasn't a total idiot. Which was why she'd agreed to the counseling class.

Molly came over and hugged her. "I know, hon."

Phoebe hugged her back, thankful for Molly's support.

With a squeeze to Phoebe's arm, Molly pulled away. "So how's it going with the sheriff's adventuresome daughter? When I came in yesterday for my ice cream fix, she didn't seem too happy to be here."

"Not so good." Phoebe headed back behind the counter, glad Heidi had filled Molly in on why she'd be working here. Phoebe didn't like hiding things from her best friend. "She's shown up the last two days looking as if she's been sentenced to hard labor for the Grinch, and any attempts I made to draw her out were shut down with sullen silences and huffy looks."

"Didn't you say when we talked on the phone the other night that she seemed pretty amenable to working here when you and Carson came up with her punishment?"

"I thought so," Phoebe said, shrugging. "But she's got a bee in her bonnet again, and her attitude is making me feel about an inch tall."

"Did you really expect her to embrace her punishment?" Molly asked with a rueful look as she plopped down in a stool opposite the counter. "C'mon. Be real."

"No." Phoebe chewed her lip. "But I thought maybe she'd loosen up a bit."

"She's twelve, Phoebs. *Loose and relaxed* isn't even in her vocabulary."

"Yeah, I guess so. I was just hoping…"

Molly quirked a brow. "That she'd instantly like you?"

Phoebe lifted one shoulder and tilted her head sideways. "Is that such a bad thing?"

"No, it's not bad. Just unrealistic."

Molly was right. Heidi was going to be a tough nut to crack. Impossible, maybe. But somehow, Phoebe felt the compelling need to at least try to work a bit of Heidi's shell loose.

"Probably," she said. "But I'm a sucker for punishment, so I'll keep trying to soften her edges."

"Knowing your kind heart, that doesn't surprise me," Molly said with a warm smile.

The bells over the door rang, and a family of tourists bustled in. Phoebe served them, glad for the distraction of the kids' smiles and beach-induced happiness.

They left with enough scoops of ice cream for three families, and Molly approached from where she'd been standing looking out the window. "I think I just saw Sheriff Winters walking by," she said, switching gears almost midthought. "He still looks mighty good in that uniform."

Phoebe's heart tripped, and before she could stop the reaction, her gaze flew to the window. "Really?"

"Wow." Molly chuckled. "Are you just a little anxious to see the man?"

Phoebe closed her eyes for a second. She had to be more careful around Molly about letting her ill-advised and unwanted interest in Carson Winters—and his uniform—show. "No. Of course not." That was the plan, and she was sticking to it.

"Really? Because for just a second it seemed like maybe you had a little…crush going on there."

The word *crush* set Phoebe on edge. "I don't do crushes," she said, her chin elevated to emphasize her point. Yes, the new sheriff in town was attractive. But his family situation was a mess. Enough said.

"There's a first time for everything," Molly said.

"Not my first."

Molly blinked. "Sorry. Right. Second," Molly said, recovering quickly.

Phoebe rolled her eyes.

"Hey, he's a hunk," Molly said, probably going for levity. "If I weren't already happily taken, *I'd* have a crush on the guy."

Phoebe sighed. "I know where this is going, Little Miss Matchmaker," she said ruefully.

"Where?" Molly asked, all innocence as usual, and playing dumb about her motives.

"Down your usual matchmaker path," Phoebe said, glaring. "The one I can't get you to step off."

"So what if I am going down that path?" Molly moved closer, then leaned a hip against the counter. "I love that path, and I'm happy where it's taken me."

Phoebe gave her a deadpan look.

"I really think you need to start dating again, and I'm sensing Sheriff Winters is the perfect guy," Molly said, ignoring Phoebe's nonverbal cue.

Phoebe shook her head at the mention of Molly's love mojo, i.e., her self-proclaimed ability to sense who belonged with whom romantically.

"Trust me when I say he's not perfect for me," Phoebe said pointedly.

"Care to tell me why? Aside from your need to avoid romance?"

Phoebe straightened the napkin and cone holder on the fountain counter. How was she going to get Molly to back off...?

Okay. She'd have to bend what she felt was a confidence between the sheriff and herself and tell Molly a bit about the Winterses' family drama, without going into specifics or gossiping. Fortunately she could trust Molly to keep whatever Phoebe told her to herself.

"He and his daughter have been through a lot, and are having major problems." She grabbed a clean sponge and cleaned an invisible spot off the counter. "The last thing I want is to get caught up in some kind of messy father/daughter crisis."

Molly jabbed a finger in the air. "Aha. No wonder you want to bond with Heidi."

Phoebe blinked.

"Because you've been through a lot, too?" Molly said, as if the reasons for her statement were obvious.

"Maybe you're right," Phoebe said, conceding the point because it was valid. "But bonding with Heidi and getting hung up on her father are two very different things."

"Yes, but—"

Phoebe kept going, needing to make her point. "And, the fact remains I'll never fall in love again, so why try?" She stared at Molly, crossing her arms over her chest. "Right?"

Molly sat silently for a moment, chewing her lip, the wheels in her head obviously turning.

"Plus, he's a cop. No way am I going to get involved with someone who works in law enforcement."

Finally she lifted a piercing green gaze to Phoebe. "I find all of this very interesting," she said in a speculative tone. "Fascinating, actually."

Phoebe scrunched her eyebrows together. "Why?" she asked, hoping Molly would spout some vague theory and then drop the subject so they could talk about flowers again.

"Because for a woman who claims to be so indifferent to Carson Winters, you've sure spent a heap of time coming up with lots of reasons why you don't want to go out with him."

"So?" Phoebe said, looking at Molly sideways.

Molly stood, cocking her head. "So, to quote someone who—I don't know—probably knew what they were talking about, 'methinks thou doth protest too much.'"

"Your point?" Phoebe asked, anticipating the worst.

"You're attracted to him, Phoebs. And that scares you to death."

"So, anything you want to talk about?"

Carson looked over his cup of black coffee at his cousin, Lily, taking careful note of the well-intentioned-on-her-part, yet dreaded-on-his-part interest in her eyes.

She was on a fishing expedition. No wonder she'd pushed him to meet for coffee at The Coffee Cabana in the middle of the afternoon.

His fingers squeezed the handle of his coffee mug. Had Heidi filled Lily in on the latest drama in the Winterses' household when she and Lily had gone shopping last night? Or was Lily just being her usual nosy, talk-to-me-I-can-help self?

Either way, Carson didn't want to get into it. "Well, Ollie Sanders got busted for ~~drunk and disorderly~~ yesterday, and Mrs. Jaquith backed her car into another fire hydrant. Oh, and it seems someone left a bag of dog doo in the middle of Pelican Lane sometime last night and Jimmy Voss called to complain that it hadn't been picked up yet—"

"I'm not talking about job stuff," Lily said, smoothing her long, blond hair behind one ear.

He stared at her, but didn't say anything. The last thing he wanted to do was rehash how Heidi had gone rogue and taken a walk on the wild side, straight to the candy bins of I Scream for Ice Cream.

What was done was done, he'd meted out punishment and that was that. Time to move on, keep the peace between him and Heidi as best he could. And hope they both made it through her teen years without driving each other crazy.

Lily took a leisurely sip of her caramel macchiato, then set her cup down and said, "I had a long talk with Heidi last night in the teen lingerie department, and she told me that things aren't going so well."

"You're really out to get me today, aren't you?"

"What are you talking about?"

"Teen *lingerie?*"

Lily chuckled. "Oh, Carson. She's not going to be a little girl forever—"

He hissed and raised a hand, cutting her off. "What did she say?"

"She told me about the ice cream parlor."

"Okay." Not surprising Heidi had shared that with Lily.

"So, she's clearly struggling."

"I know." He took a sip of his coffee, hating that he had to agree with her. "But I've dealt with what she did with a consequence, and she's apologized to Phoebe Sellers. Everything's been handled."

"You really think it's that easy?"

He looked at the swirling blackness of the coffee in his cup and remained silent. He didn't want this turmoil.

After a bit of a silence, Lily said, "Carson, Heidi has been dealt two terrible blows, and she's acting out because she's having a hard time dealing with all the changes in her life."

"I get it." That much was obvious. But what to do about the obvious? Not quite so much a slam dunk.

Maybe he needed help here. He hated asking, but for Heidi's sake, he would. "Any suggestions?" he asked, slanting a glance at Lily.

She leaned forward. "Have you thought about getting her counseling?"

Guilt zapped him. "I haven't had time to find someone." Yeah, he'd dropped the ball on that one. But keeping all of the balls in the air on his own since they'd moved had been a real challenge.

"Why don't you let me work on finding a good teen therapist around here, okay?"

He nodded stiffly.

"And how about more counseling for yourself?" Lily asked, regarding him directly. "I can't imagine the few sessions the department required were enough."

"I'm fine," he said curtly. But was he really?

She leaned in and touched his hand. "No one would be fine after everything that's happened to you."

"I can handle it." And he would. Somehow. That's what he did—plodded on without complaint and dealt.

"Yeah, I know you think you can." She quirked her mouth. "But you're a guy, and most guys just want to put their heads down and plow forward."

"Yep, that pretty much sums it up right there." And if he could avoid emotional chaos, even better.

"So. How's that working for you?"

He shifted in his chair and ground his molars together. "Not that well," he said truthfully. Heidi deserved that he be honest with himself. Even if he didn't like dissecting every little emotion. Or admitting he needed help.

Lily picked up her purse. She dug around inside, then pulled out a piece of folded green paper and held it out for him. "Take a look at this. I picked it up at church last Sunday."

Wary, he took the paper and unfolded it, scanning the contents quickly. His stomach pitched.

The flyer announced a series of classes set to take place at Moonlight Cove Community Church every Thursday night for the next month. Starting tonight.

Grief-counseling classes.

Sighing heavily, he dropped the paper on the table and looked at Lily. "You really think this will help?"

"Yes, I do. You're grieving the death of your son and the death of your marriage. That's a lot for anyone to deal with, Carson. Someone would have to be a superhero to handle what's happened on their own."

"I thought I *was* a superhero," he said, his voice rough. "I've always been able to handle life's ups and downs on my own." Although he'd never been thrown something as traumatic as his son dying and his wife abandoning him.

"I know, and you've been superhuman in the past, believe me. But that routine isn't working now, and your daughter is struggling. Don't you think you need to get some help to deal with your grief—to heal—so you can give her what she needs and deserves?"

More guilt loaded on. How could he have gone so wrong? "Everything you've said is true," he said. "But honestly, Lily, this feels like a failure to me." He let out a derisive snort. "I should be able to handle this without some class to show me the way."

She looked at him, understanding in her brown eyes. "It's not a sign of weakness to ask for help."

"It is in my book," he replied, swiping a rigid hand through his hair. "I'm a cop, a problem solver. I'm used to stress. I should be able to deal."

"Well, you're going to need to get over that misconception for Heidi's sake."

For Heidi's sake.

Those words reverberated in him, hitting home Lily's point like brass knuckles to the gut. He needed to focus on what was best for Heidi, and she needed him, now more than ever. He'd be a selfish idiot and a neglectful parent not to see that and act on it.

"I'll do whatever I have to for Heidi," he said to Lily. Even if doing so meant admitting his weaknesses and attending some touchy-feely counseling class for the next four weeks.

Even though he rather be Tasered, what other choice did he have?

"So," Rebecca, the grief-counseling instructor, said from the front of the room. "Does anyone have any questions?"

Phoebe shifted in the small, hard chair set up in a classroom in the basement of the Moonlight Cove Community Church. Thankfully the rest of the grief-management classes would take place in the more comfortable singles'-group lounge, once that room became available next week. Spending any more time in these uncomfortable chairs didn't really float her boat.

Someone to her left raised their hand and asked about the schedule. Phoebe tapped her pencil on the desk, listening intently, trying to make the most of her time here, even though she'd had to coerce herself to come.

Forcing herself to talk about painful things was always, well, painful, and she felt like she had when she'd gone to the dentist for a root canal.

Fortunately, they had Novocain for a root canal. But for handling grief? No such thing.

When all of the questions had been answered, Rebecca said, "All right. I've gone over the basic structure of the course and covered the schedule in depth. Now, if you'll remember, I mentioned working with a discussion partner outside of class."

Everyone in the class murmured their assent along with Phoebe.

"Okay, there are twelve of us, and since Randy and Joanna are married and want to be partners, we'll need to count off by fives to make five groups of two." She pointed right. "Start here and count off, and then we'll partner up, get to know each other for a few minutes, and adjourn."

Everyone dutifully said their number, and Phoebe uttered "five" when it was her turn. The counting hit the back of the room, and the last person to speak—a guy with a vaguely familiar deep voice—said "five" after a pause. The counting ended.

Phoebe drew her eyebrows together. She hadn't noticed any men in the very back of the room when the class had started…

Gathering up her things, she stood and turned around to see who she'd be working with. Only to be met with the dark, piercing, none-too-happy yet surprised gaze of Sheriff Carson Winters.

She blinked as her heart tripped over itself. Freezing in midmotion as she slung her purse over her shoulder, she almost whacked the woman standing next to her.

Oh, no. What was he doing at a *grief*-counseling class? His wife had left him and Heidi, yes. Did death of a marriage count? Probably so…

A new depth of empathy grabbed ahold of her and twisted. Automatically, a prayer rose inside of her. *Lord, please help the Winterses through this, and give them the strength they'll need to heal. And help me, too, please. I think I'm going to need it.*

Because as a woman out to keep her life on an even track, spending any one-on-one time with the compelling Carson Winters was the very last thing she wanted to do.

Chapter Four

"So, it looks like we're discussion partners."

As Phoebe spoke, Carson arranged his face in a neutral expression and smothered the need to snort.

Figured he'd get paired up with the pretty blonde, who looked even nicer than he remembered, dressed in a black belted coat, jeans and hot-pink scarf that really played up the blue in her eyes.

Actually, getting paired up with anybody wasn't exactly thrilling him; he'd been planning on dutifully sitting through some lectures, maybe filling out some forms or something. *Alone.* He hadn't counted on sharing himself—or his feelings—with anyone.

Especially not the engaging ice-cream-store owner.

Belatedly, he realized that Phoebe was obviously here because she was dealing with grief herself. What was her story, anyway? And why was he so interested?

He rolled a shoulder. "Yep, looks like we are."

A pause. "You don't look too happy about being here," she said, hitching her purse up.

Guess he was a bad actor. "I'm not."

"Yeah, I get that," she said, surprising him. "I promised my mom I'd come, and…well, let's just say it's hard saying no to her."

Again, his interest flared; who was she grieving? Guess he'd find out soon enough. "Then we're in the same boat."

She looked at him questioningly.

"I promised Lily I'd come," he said.

"Ah. I see."

"But I'd never have come of my own volition. I'm not much of a talker." Especially when it came to what ailed him.

She nodded, biting her lip. "Look, if you'd rather have another partner…"

"I didn't want *any* partner," he said, his jaw ticking. "So don't be offended."

Her mouth thinned. "Well, *that* makes me feel better."

He sighed. "I'm handling this badly, aren't I?"

"Pretty much," she replied, nodding.

"Sorry." He laughed under his breath. "This kind of stuff isn't my strong point." Susan had always said he was a bad interpersonal communicator and liked to hold things close to the vest. She'd been wrong about a lot of things, but right about that; he'd been raised to keep his chin up, no matter what.

"I don't think anyone likes talking about painful stuff," Phoebe said, softly, her eyes shimmering. "Especially grief."

Before he could respond to Phoebe's comment, Rebecca clapped her hands. The class quieted and all eyes looked her way.

"While you're talking with your partner, please discuss why you're here, all right?" Rebecca said. "That way, everyone will be on the same page, and no one will have to ask an insensitive question. And feel free to go somewhere more comfortable to talk. Class is over for tonight. See you all next week."

Phoebe turned to him, her eyebrows raised. "You want to spill first?"

His throat burned. "Quite frankly, no." Rebecca's suggestion to share their history made sense, but he honestly didn't know how he could even utter CJ's name without crumbling.

Without reliving his failure.

"Yeah. Me, neither," Phoebe said ruefully. "Looks like we're at an impasse."

Other members of the class began filing out, although a few stayed, talking in small groups. Rebecca, who'd been making the rounds, walked up.

"How's it going, you two?" she asked.

"Not so good," Phoebe said. "We both feel…awkward about sharing."

That was putting it mildly.

"That's natural, completely normal," Rebecca replied. "This opening-up process frequently feels wrong and problematic at first."

She had that right. Sharing his agony felt so not right, so against his natural instincts to keep everything within himself. His gut told him to clam up and ignore his feelings and hope they just went away.

Rebecca leaned against a desk. "Dealing with grief is difficult, no doubt about it."

Exactly. Handling CJ's death had been the hardest challenge Carson had ever come up against. And that was saying a lot, given his occupation.

Continuing on, Rebecca said, "But you guys came to the class to get help in that endeavor, right?"

He and Phoebe nodded.

"Well, then, if you're ever going to heal, you're going to need to get to a place where you can talk about what you're going through, how you're feeling."

Her words echoed what Lily had told him at the coffee shop earlier today, and that, in turn, reminded him of why he was here—for Heidi. For her, he needed to man up in a way that felt foreign to him, and deal instead of doing his usual routine of burying his head in the sand. And that meant forcing himself to go through the process Rebecca was laying out before them.

He looked at Phoebe. "You game?"

"I don't know."

"Do you think you can tough it out for your mom's sake? You made it through the door."

"I did." She twitched her lips. "Yeah, I can tough it out for her."

"Okay, then."

She raised an eyebrow at him. "For Heidi?"

"For Heidi," he said, even though he felt the walls of

the small basement meeting room closing in on him, trapping him in a place akin to facing a lowlife with a gun, his own back against the wall.

Rebecca piped in. "You always have a choice. You just have to decide which choice is in your and your loved ones' best interest. In short, which path will lead you to a better place?"

And more importantly, which path would help Heidi? Because acting in Heidi's best interest was what he was all about. Always.

"Gotcha," he said, then turned his attention to Phoebe. "I'll give this discussion thing my best shot, but this place is getting claustrophobic. What do you say we go and talk over a cup of joe?"

Phoebe hesitated, her blue eyes reflecting what looked similar to the same unease he was feeling. After a few beats, she drew in a breath and said, "Sounds like a plan. Let's go."

They said goodbye to Rebecca and he followed his new discussion partner out into the cool evening, belatedly wondering how smart it was to spend any personal time with the lovely Phoebe Sellers.

Or to share his grief and pain when he suspected doing so would feel as if he was yanking his heart out all over again.

The Coffee Cabana was closing in half an hour, so it was deserted when Carson held the door open for Phoebe and she stepped inside the place.

Inhaling the scent of fresh ground coffee, she waved

to Blake Stonely, the thirty-something owner who'd bought the place last year, and then grabbed the first table by the door, feeling the need to not be tucked away in some intimate corner with Mr. Cute Sheriff.

Carson took off his hat and set it on the extra chair at the table she'd chosen. "What can I get you?" he asked.

He'd insisted on paying for her coffee when they'd arrived on foot at The Coffee Cabana, Moonlight Cove's own little version of coffee and pastry paradise.

Phoebe looked up at him and automatically said, "Coffee, black, thanks." She was gonna need fortification to get through this meeting.

However…maybe the caffeine was a bad idea if she was actually planning on sleeping tonight. Which she was. "Actually, make that a decaf, would you?"

He nodded and headed up to the counter to order.

She watched him go, her eyes lingering on his broad shoulders and narrow waist, again noticing that he walked with a natural economy of movement she found attractive. Ripping her gaze away from him, she admonished herself for noticing anything about him at all. She had bigger things to focus on here.

Such as getting stuck with him as her discussion partner. Well, not stuck, exactly. He was a nice guy and all, and would probably make someone else an excellent sounding board. But did it have to be her?

She'd already promised herself to stay disengaged from the Winters family. This little situation hardly qualified. Carson would be privy to her untidy business before long, and he'd know all about Justin. And her personal heartbreak.

She unbuttoned her coat, telling herself to calm down, to keep perspective. This new development wasn't the end of the world. She should know; she'd lived through the seeming end of her world when Justin had died. No contest here.

Okay. So. Everything was fine. She needed to relax and go with the flow and, as Rebecca had said, respect the process. To heal the wound on her heart, she had to make a choice that wasn't comfortable—*how true*— but that would lead her to a better, more settled place. Eventually.

Besides, she'd already told Carson she was game if he was, and it wouldn't be cool to ditch him now because she was an emotional wimp.

She straightened the sweetener holder, then jiggled her foot under the table, waiting for him to return, going over what she needed to do in the next twenty minutes.

Loosen up. She stopped shaking her foot.

Talk. She cleared her throat and opened her mind to sharing what had happened to her.

Listen. She steeled herself to hear about Carson's story.

Deal. Tricky. But, hopefully, not impossible.

Carson came back with two cups of coffee and two apple tarts, complete with whipped cream and caramel drizzle. "Thought you might be interested in something sweet," he said, putting her coffee and treat, along with some utensils, on the table before her.

She blinked, her mouth watering. "How did you know those are my favorite?"

"I didn't." He sat and grabbed a napkin from the napkin holder. "They just looked good."

He obviously had his sweet-tooth priorities in excellent order. "Trust me, they are," she said, picking up one of the forks. "I've actually thought about offering some kind of ice cream based on these."

"That sounds like it would be a big hit."

"I know." She dug into the pastry, carefully mixing just the right amount of apples, flaky crust and whipped cream.

"Maybe with a caramel swirl?" he asked.

"Of course," she said, toasting him with a big bite before she popped it in her mouth. Delicious.

He took a sip of his coffee, which looked hot and black, no embellishments. Ah. A man after her own coffee heart. Good thing a love for black coffee and apple tarts was all they had in common. Except, she firmly reminded herself, the reason they were here.

To discuss their respective losses.

Her foot started going again, and suddenly her appetite crashed and burned. She put her fork down and took a sip of her coffee. And then another, wishing now she'd gone with the caffeine.

Carson looked up from making quick work of his tart. He stopped chewing for a moment, then continued on and swallowed. "So, how's it going with Heidi at the parlor?" he asked after a sip of coffee.

That was a safe subject to start. Great. Her leg relaxed. "She's been a bit...prickly," she said, choosing a kind word so Carson wouldn't freak out.

"Prickly? Or rude?" he asked, his gaze laser sharp.

Phoebe shifted in her seat. "Not rude. Just...standoffish."

He sighed heavily, shaking his head. "I thought her attitude had cooled down a bit."

"Yeah, she gave me that impression, too, when the three of us met in my office. But for whatever reason, she's definitely giving off a sullen vibe."

"I'll talk to her—"

"No, don't," Phoebe said, holding up a hand. "I want to work this out myself, and I certainly don't want Heidi thinking we're talking behind her back."

"But we are."

"True. But no matter how we twist it, it'll seem like we're ganging up on her, and that's the last thing I want. Just let me figure this out on my own, all right?"

"Fine," he allowed. "But I want you to tell me if she keeps up the attitude."

"I promise," Phoebe said.

Silence stretched out, and Phoebe's leg started twitching again. She clamped a hand down on her thigh, to no avail.

He frowned and then leaned sideways and looked underneath the table. Straightening, his brows raised, he said, "Let me make a wild guess and assume you're nervous about…talking."

"You could say that." Despite her best efforts to the contrary. "Sometimes knowing what I need to do is easier than actually doing it."

"Meaning?"

"Well, I know I need to relax and embrace the process, but actually starting this discussion is proving to be…difficult."

She went on. "Talking about…what happened… has never been easy for me," Phoebe shoved out. Molly was the only one she'd ever really opened up to. Mainly because Molly was just pushy enough to wear her down.

Carson shifted in his seat. "I wouldn't normally ask, but I guess we have to go there." He paused. "What *did* happen?"

Eyes tingling, throat thick, she bit her lip and blinked rapidly, though any attempt at stemming the waterworks was probably futile. "Someone I loved died."

His gaze darted to his coffee cup. He looked back up, his eyes brimming with sympathy. "Who?"

"My fiancé."

He hissed out a breath. "Oh, Phoebe. I am so sorry."

Clearing her throat, she replied, "Yeah, it was a shock." She picked up her fork and started smoothing the whipped cream on top of her tart, unable to meet Carson's gaze. "He, um…was a firefighter on a Hotshot crew, and two weeks before we were supposed to get married he was killed in a wildfire in central Oregon." Tears welled and crested.

"How long ago was this?"

"Two years." She grabbed a napkin and dabbed at her eyes from the bottom rim up, trying not to smudge her mascara, though it was probably pointless. For the first six weeks after Justin had died, she hadn't even bothered putting on makeup because she just cried it off by midmorning.

"Wow. That must have been rough," Carson said.

"It's the worst thing that's ever happened to me."

He sat for a moment, just shaking his head, his mouth pressed into a tight line. He took a sip of his coffee, then fiddled with his fork. "Having someone you love die is…awful," he finally said, his voice rough and streaked with deep sadness and obvious empathy that told her he knew firsthand what she'd gone through. And suddenly she was certain he was talking about more than just the death of his marriage.

"You lost someone you loved, didn't you? Someone besides your wife," she stated in a hoarse whisper, afraid to hear his answer.

He nodded, a single, jerky motion of his head that spoke volumes.

A rock formed in her gut, sending physical pain flashing through her to mingle with the emotional pain that had been with her ever since Justin had died.

It was obvious she was in over her head with this whole discussion thing. Dealing with her own grief was bad enough. But to have to hear about Carson's, and handle whatever he shared with her?

She wasn't sure she could do it.

But then she saw the sadness and loss emanating from his eyes. Gutting up, she shoved down the need to bolt. She'd agreed to this, and she instinctively knew she'd have to walk through fire now to help herself, and him, in the long run.

Because helping him with his grief was important to her. There was that softy part of her taking over again. And right now, she wished that part of herself would take a hike. Even so, she couldn't deny that mushy part existed any more than she could deny she had blue eyes.

"Tell me who it was," she forced out, making herself look directly at him when all she really wanted to do was memorize the wood-grain pattern on the table in front of her and then straighten every napkin holder in sight.

He closed his eyes and his mouth trembled, and she thought she'd lose it right then and there. Steeling herself, she patiently waited for him to speak.

He pressed a hand to the bridge of his nose, and then sucked in a large breath. "My son," he said in a jagged, agonized whisper. "I lost my boy, and nothing will ever be the same."

All Phoebe heard was the sound of her heart shattering.

Chapter Five

As soon as the words about CJ left Carson's mouth, he saw Phoebe freeze, her glimmering eyes chock-full of raw empathy tinged with horror. Perhaps a bit of denial?

No one wanted to hear about or accept the death of a child.

Clearly, though, she understood his tragedy on a deeply personal level. She'd lost someone important, too. Her fiancé. The man she'd loved. *Still* loved, he was sure. A woman like Phoebe wouldn't just stop loving. No way. Not in a million years.

Carson's chest squeezed. No one should have to go through what they'd been through.

Unable to watch the play of emotions on her face—he'd felt every one of them a multitude of times since CJ died—he focused intently on picking up his coffee cup and taking a sip, hoping the strong brew would ease the tightness in his chest.

He remained silent. Not sure what to say, he felt

awkward and out of his league. As though he wanted to be anywhere but here with this charming woman, talking about the worst things that had ever happened to both of them.

Had he lost his mind?

Then, unexpectedly, she reached out and squeezed his hand, her fingers lingering on his. "I can't tell you how sorry I am."

Warmth flared where her fingers rested, and he instantly wanted to curl his hand around hers and hold on. Her touch, all warm and soft, was, he knew, meant to be comforting.

Yep, there went his marbles…

But in the split second it took to recover his sanity, he realized her touch made him edgy; wanting to "hold on" to Phoebe Sellers in any way, shape or form brought to light a potentially dangerous bond he wanted no part of.

"Thank you," was all he could manage.

She fiddled with her fork, then started smoothing the whipped cream on her tart again. Finally, she said, "Do you want to tell me what happened?"

He made a rough sound under his breath. "Not really," he said, going with his gut.

"Loss is hard to talk about, isn't it?" Phoebe said, leaning in slightly, her clear blue eyes soft with compassion.

"Impossible." He'd relived that day in his mind, in his nightmares, countless times. He wasn't sure he could go there willingly and actually *speak* about his part in CJ's death. About his unforgivable failure as a man, a father and a cop. Every man in him had failed CJ.

Susan had realized that.

"Hey, I hear you there," Phoebe said. "Ever since Justin died, the only person I've been able to talk to about his death is Molly." Phoebe rolled her eyes and quirked her mouth. "And that's only because she's pushy that way—which, I suppose, is a good thing."

"I've never talked about…that day," he admitted.

"It's hard to force ourselves to confront our grief," she said. "And it's hard for others to ask us about it. I can't tell you how many people saw me after Justin died and just said nothing."

He slowly nodded. "To this day my best friend on the force hasn't spoken to me." He gritted his jaw, still feeling Rick's abandonment like a switchblade shoved in and twisted, then shoved in farther. "Not a call, email, text, nothing."

Phoebe shook her head. "Guess it's human nature."

"He didn't even come to CJ's funeral." Carson cleared his throat. Stupid frog, living there. "That really slayed me."

"I'm sure," Phoebe said, empathy reflected in her eyes, tinged with a strength he was struggling to have himself. "He was your best friend."

Of course, on one level in Carson's mind, he'd understood Rick's reaction. What did one cop say to another who'd been responsible for his own kid's death?

Nothing, that's what. There were no words. No forgiveness or understanding or comfort or absolution.

The familiar nausea rolled through him. "Yeah, well, we're not friends anymore," he said in a monotone. "Another loss, another problem to deal with." He snorted. "No wonder Heidi's been acting out."

Just then, Blake came up to the table. "Hey, Sheriff, Phoebe. Sorry to interrupt your discussion, but store's closing in a few."

Phoebe raised a hand. "Thanks, Blake."

With a wave, Blake headed back behind the front counter.

Phoebe stood, coffee cup in hand, and turned to leave. Carson grabbed his hat and followed her out the door and onto the boardwalk. The sun had almost set, and the sky to the west was covered in orange and red streaks. The clouds had cleared, and Carson could see the stars twinkling overhead. The weather forecast called for sunny skies tomorrow, and it was a Friday. With the nice weather and the usual summer weekend tourists hitting town, work would be busy for the next few days.

Phoebe walked beside him, silent. He stayed quiet, too, taking her cue. But he was very aware of her significant presence next to him.

What was it about her that attracted him so? He'd need to figure it out soon, or risk more mental turmoil.

She turned to him. "What did you mean by 'no wonder Heidi's been acting out'?"

He slowly put his hat back on and adjusted it, stalling, figuring out how to reply. Finally, he said, "Just that with all our struggles lately, Heidi probably thinks she's got a loser for a dad."

Phoebe frowned. "Loser?"

"You know. Someone weak who can't deal." Which had been him lately. Man, he hated feeling so clueless. So needy. Not the invincible man he wanted to be.

"You think you're a weak loser?" Phoebe asked, looking askance at him.

"I've realized in the last few days, what with Heidi and all, that I haven't been able to handle...what happened very well." As in *not at all*.

Phoebe just looked at him, as if she were expecting more.

He delivered. "To me, *handling it* means moving on without a lot of unnecessary hoo-ha." He let out a harsh sigh. "That's what I'd been trying to do, but it turns out I have more hoo-ha than I know what to do with."

"Sounds to me like you're being too hard on yourself."

"Maybe," he said, shrugging. "But that's just the way I operate." Always had been. While he loved his parents, and had a good relationship with them, and they visited every year from Spokane, his folks had never been demonstrative people, or even talkative, at least about problems. His dad was a cop's cop with a very traditional mentality; Carson and his sister, Lynne, had been raised to carry on. Spine ramrod straight. No complaining.

"Well, maybe you need to operate differently," Phoebe said.

"Lily said essentially the same thing. But I am who I am, and admitting I need…help?" His stubborn side had him wagging his head. "That I can't handle things?" Another wag. "Well, that doesn't come easy."

She stopped by one of the benches on the boardwalk about a block from her store. The streetlight from above highlighted her pretty face's delicate bone structure.

"I understand what you're saying. After losing Justin, I struggle with admitting I need anyone, too." She pressed her lips together and looked down for a moment. When she looked back up, her eyes glowed with a compelling softness that was evident, even in the dark. "But you've been dealt two terrible blows. You're entitled to have trouble dealing, if you ask me."

Rather than stir up the pot, he just stared at her blankly.

She pursed her lips, staring back. After a few long moments, she said wryly, "Going for the strong, silent type, huh?"

"What do you want me to say?"

She raised her chin and peered at him. "Okay. Fine. Just listen."

He crossed his arms over his chest and nodded slightly.

"Although," she said, giving him a mildly deprecating look, "it might be good if you uncrossed your arms and actually tried to appear nondefensive."

He obliged her with a nod and uncrossed his arms, letting them dangle at his sides.

"So, do you view me as weak?" she asked.

"No." At least not what he'd seen so far, which, admittedly, wasn't much. But he had good people instincts—most good cops did. "You strike me as a very strong woman." Actually, he liked that about her.

"Well, thank you," she said with a slight incline of her head. "But the truth is, I'm having a hard time dealing, too, or I wouldn't have come to the class tonight."

He nodded, taking her at her word, although to outward appearances it seemed as if she was handling her grief better than he was.

But…he was always hardest on himself.

Holding up an index finger, she said, "So, in your world, since I'm having a hard time dealing, that makes me weak."

"No—"

"What do you mean, *no?*"

He blinked.

"I'm just applying your principle to myself," she said with a raised eyebrow.

Her statement took him aback, and he didn't know how to respond.

She plopped down on the bench. "So why are you weak, but I'm not?"

Tricky gal, that Phoebe. He'd have to watch that or she'd be running him in circles before he knew it. "Gotta ask the tough questions, don't you?"

"I'm just feeling my way here, but apparently that's my job as your discussion partner."

His discomfort rose, so he lowered himself to sit next to her. She didn't scoot over to give him more room. She wasn't the type to give an inch. He smiled a little.

"You're not going to cut me any breaks, are you?" he said.

"No, I'm not," she said, turning so she faced him. "And you know why?"

"Fire away." She was on a roll, and he sensed there was no stopping her.

"I'm not cutting you any breaks because…" Her voice broke. "Because I know you're sad, I know you probably think your life is never going to be happy again."

He looked at her and saw the sudden tears shining in her eyes. Saw his own pain and suffering reflected there. His throat tightened and he had to look away or he'd lose it.

"You know why I know this?" she asked, her voice whispering over him in the darkness, a feather with an edge that had the power to cut him to shreds.

Of course he knew. But he couldn't bring himself to say the words. Or acknowledge out loud the bond she was alluding to.

When he didn't respond, she said, "Because I feel that way, too, and I see myself in you."

He closed his eyes and let his shoulders slump, wanting to deny her statement with everything in him.

But he couldn't, not really; they shared the same grief, the same sense of loss, the same fears.

She understood him. Or had the potential to.

And that would cut him clean and deep if he got caught up in the bond he shared with Phoebe Sellers.

Phoebe saw Carson close his eyes, saw him sag under the weight of his sorrow, and her heart went out to him.

She fought the urge to put her arms around him and comfort him, take on some of his burden, if that were possible.

Her touch—sympathetic or otherwise—was probably the last thing he wanted right now. Or ever.

Right. She had to remember that. Because she felt the same way, too, didn't she?

Instead, she let him sit in silence and absorb what she'd said, to adjust to the prospect of sharing his grief. Or at least consider doing so.

While she waited for him to respond, one thought slashed through her brain: How could a parent possibly bear the death of a child? If she were him... well, she probably would have curled up and died in a corner by now.

Not surprising, then, that he seemed reluctant to talk, to open up. She felt his hesitation, felt the discomfort that rolled off him in waves much like the water cresting and crashing onto the shore just a block away. He was, of course, entitled; it had to be agony for him to talk about his son's death.

Given that reality, she wouldn't be surprised if he clammed up and shut down. For Heidi's sake, Phoebe hoped he didn't; Heidi had lost her brother and her mother. Phoebe couldn't even imagine how crushing those two back-to-back blows must have been.

Heidi needed her dad to be emotionally healthy so she could deal with the tragedies that had struck recently.

Who wouldn't need that? Carson included.

And…herself, too? Hard questions? Definitely.

Finally, Carson sat up and set his jaw. "I don't think I can have this discussion," he said, confirming Phoebe's hunch.

Phoebe was oddly disappointed by his response, yet understood it implicitly. "I thought you might say that."

"Why?"

"As I said before, it's never easy to talk about the things that have hurt us; it's a natural reaction to avoid pain."

"I'm just going with my gut here."

"Trust me, I'm guilty of the same thing, just ask Molly. She thinks I'm the biggest ostrich of all." Especially since Molly had opened her own eyes to love recently.

He scrunched his brows together.

"You know." She tapped her head. "Because I bury my head in the sand?"

"Ah. Interesting analogy." He shifted on the bench. "But only accurate to a point."

She threw him a puzzled glance.

"I fully acknowledge the truth of my life," he said. "So while the ostrich comment is right on one level, as in yes, ostriches bury their heads—at least in cartoons—I don't see myself as an ostrich, per se."

"Say what?" she said with a twitch of her chin. "You lost me."

He sighed. "I'm not hiding from the truth."

"You're not?"

"Nope." He sat pensively for a moment. "I'm more of a…bear."

"Care to explain?"

"Sure. A bear does what he needs to survive, and gets along fine without analyzing everything to death. Hence, the bear isn't burying his head in the sand. He's just doing his bear thing, on his own, and that works for him."

"You mean, the bear's in denial," she said wryly.

"No, he's not, because he isn't denying the reality of his life. He's just dealing with his reality in his own way, with his paws and his teeth, like a bear is supposed to."

She blinked, taken about by his logic.

"I can see I've given you food for thought." He got up and held out his hand for her to rise. "With that, I'll say good-night."

She took his hand and stood, a bit thrown by the contact, as well as his clever and remarkably insightful comeback. Thinking fast, she said, "I guess we'll have to agree to disagree, then."

"We could, but I'm not sure we really disagree," he said. "Do you think so?"

Trouble was, she didn't.

Phoebe needed to finish up some paperwork, so Carson escorted her the block or so to her store after their discussion by the bench.

As they walked in thoughtful silence, nodding to the people enjoying the evening on the boardwalk, he had to admit he was spinning; Phoebe had brought up some tough subject matter, for sure.

Subject matter that ripped him up inside.

As a self-described bear, he didn't much like the feeling. Chances were, talking to Phoebe wouldn't get any easier. Eventually, she'd wear him down, and not only would he have to pick apart his pain, he'd see her pain firsthand, too.

And he'd have to admit to his failure.

Warning sirens blared in his head.

He saw a plump, gray-haired woman coming toward him on the boardwalk. Recognizing his deputy's mom, Ruby Diaz, Carson waved, looking for all the world as if he and Phoebe were just out for a casual stroll, enjoying the lovely evening.

What a pretty illusion.

He was feeling anything but casual as he reiterated to himself that, yes, he was willing to sit through a relatively impersonal class. But pouring out his guts to perceptive, attractive, charming Phoebe, while she did the same?

Not a good place for him to go. He'd find another way to deal.

She turned when they reached her store. "Well, this is me. Thanks for walking me here."

He nodded, clearing his throat. "No problem. Listen, as I've been alluding to, I'm really not sure if this discussion plan is my thing. I didn't sign up for one-on-ones. No offense." He adjusted his hat. "I'm good with the class, listening, you know. But this?" He motioned between them. "It's not going to work for me."

"Okay," she said after a pause. "I get where you're coming from. As I said before, talking about losing someone you loved isn't easy."

"Right." Trouble was, talking about CJ dying was so much more than just difficult for him; speaking of the tragic decisions he'd made that life-changing day was agony.

Phoebe smoothed her hair back behind one ear. "So...I respect your decision, but I don't necessarily agree with it."

Expected. "Okay."

"We're going with one-word answers now?" she asked, hoisting up one brow.

He shrugged. How better to shut down the conversation? "Guess so. That's two words, though."

She held up her hands. "Okay, okay, I get the message. I won't push."

"Thank you."

Looking right at him, her eyes as soft as blue sky,

she said, "But if you change your mind, you know where to find me."

He nodded, even though he wouldn't change his mind. "Appreciated." He had no doubt Phoebe would be there for him if he needed her. Was that a good thing, or a bad thing? Funny how the two ends of the spectrum blurred at times.

With a frustrated shake of her head and a small wave, she opened the door to her shop and disappeared inside. The door closed with a click, and she turned the OPEN sign over so it read CLOSED. She moved to the windows and closed the blinds one by one until she disappeared from view completely.

And then he was standing by himself, outside looking in. By himself by choice.

And necessarily alone with his agony that would be his own private pain, never to be shared, his own solitary burden that he had no choice but to bear as a man, a father and as a cop.

Wasn't that the least he deserved?

Chapter Six

The day after Phoebe and Carson talked on the board-walk and he'd bailed on her, Phoebe spent most of the early afternoon immersed in boring yet necessary paperwork while Tanya handled the steady flow of customers out front.

Well, Phoebe had been kinda sorta immersed in work. Unfortunately, a good chunk of her thoughts were consumed with worrying about Carson's decision to nix their discussion sessions.

It was obvious that he was in major bear denial, and she couldn't help but think that his decision to back out was a mistake. For him and daughter bear, at least.

But for herself?

Well…probably not a bad thing. Though the empathetic streak in her had her feeling a strong need to help him deal with the tragic death of his son—what person with a shred of a heart wouldn't?—in reality, getting personally involved with the Winterses wasn't a great idea.

If she had any kind of sense, she needed to quash her empathy and relegate herself to the friendly woman who owned the place on Main Street with the yummy ice cream and candy.

Nothing more.

That role had always suited her fine in the past. No need to change things, no matter how much she might be tempted to.

Maybe she should get out a big, black permanent marker and write the words *BACK AWAY FROM THE HANDSOME SHERIFF AND HIS DAUGHTER* on her hand to remind herself to stay uninvolved in Carson and Heidi's lives. She'd be smarter to focus on her own struggles. Why ask for trouble?

Sometime after lunch, during a lull of the good-weather-at-the-coast Friday customer rush, she went out front while Tanya went to lunch.

Just after Tanya left, the bells over the door jingled. Phoebe looked up from smoothing the top of the cookie-dough ice cream, pleased to see her brother, Drew. He was dressed in a tan sport coat and dark blue pants, his tie loose around his neck.

"Hey, you," she said, coming out from behind the counter. "To what do I owe this honor?"

He ran his fingers through his short brown hair. "I was in the neighborhood for a business appointment, so I thought I'd stop by and fill you in on what's going on with me."

She raised a brow. "That sounds interesting." Drew was in the midst of a bit of a career crisis; the downturn in the economy had been brutal on the real-estate business he and Dad ran together. Things had been tense between the two Sellers men for a long time— since Drew was a teen, actually, and had expressed interest in *not* taking over Dad's real-estate firm in favor of a career in firefighting—and the prospect of the family business failing hadn't helped the stress level between father and son at all. In fact, unfortunately, things had never been worse between her brother and her dad.

"It is." He sat on the end stool. "I've decided to apply to the Portland Fire Department for a full-time job, and I hope to get my paramedic certification as soon as I get a job."

"That's great," she said. Drew was a volunteer firefighter in the Moonlight Cove fire department, but his dream had always been to be a full-time paramedic in a larger city. She quirked her lips. "Although, I'm sure Dad doesn't see it that way."

"Yeah, well, that would be an understatement," he said, rubbing his shadowed jaw. "But it's time for me to quit trying to please him and do what I've wanted to do all along." This was a familiar theme for Drew, even though he'd never been able to assert himself against Dad enough to actually break free and follow his heart. Maybe the time was right for him to move on.

"About time," she said, squeezing his arm. "Any idea when you might be moving?"

"Not really. They only hire a few times a year. But

I'm hoping to get accepted to the academy on the next hiring cycle, which is a month away."

"Well, good luck, bro." Hopefully once Drew settled down into the life he wanted as a firefighter, he'd be more open to love. It was no secret that his college sweetheart had broken his heart when she'd run off with an Italian exchange student. In Phoebe's opinion, Drew would be a lot happier with a wife and a family. Something more than just a job and a few nights a month socializing at Moonlight Cove Community Church's singles' group.

Funny how she wished for things for him she didn't expect for herself....

Veering away from that enlightening thought, she asked him about his best friend, Seth, who owned The Sports Shack just down Main Street. Rumor had it that since Seth had married Kim Hampton and become a family man, he was expanding the business to Seattle. Speculation also was rife that his younger brother, Curt, was going to come to Moonlight Cove to run the store, while Seth got things rolling in Seattle.

Drew told her he was pretty sure The Sports Shack would be expanding and that Curt was on board to come to town to help out. And then, with a glance to his watch, Drew said he had to hustle to a meeting with a prospective client.

Phoebe said goodbye, and after he left, she vowed to keep her mind off Carson. To that end, she busily moved the tables and chairs, noting with a glance outside that it looked as though the whole weekend was shaping up to be busy. Sunshine and relatively warm temperatures always brought out the tourists looking for a day or weekend of sand, surf and windblown fun.

She stepped back, tapping her chin, studying the triangular setup she'd come up with, noting the angles and overall appeal of the new arrangement of tables with a critical eye.

Nope. Wasn't working. She liked it better the old way.

Just as she started to move everything back, the bells over the door jingled and Heidi walked into the store, bringing the ocean-scented breeze with her. Phoebe glanced at the clock on the wall. Was it that late already?

Heidi wore a pair of denim capris, tennis shoes and a black zip-up sweatshirt with a hood. She had her long blond hair pulled up into a ponytail, and a hot-pink backpack hung from one shoulder.

She was a pretty girl, save for the sullen expression she wore, which just made her appear rude instead of the bored and worldly she'd probably been going for. She looked as if she wasn't any happier to be here than she had been when she'd arrived yesterday, and the day before, and Phoebe had put her to work cleaning the back room to within an inch of its life.

Phoebe, however, was willing to cut her a break for her attitude and give her some time to come around. After the tragic losses Heidi had suffered, it was no wonder the girl was unhappy and acted it.

She'd really been put through a mental meat grinder,

poor thing. She and her dad really had a lot on their plates. More than one family should have to deal with.

Sympathy welled, and Phoebe had the urge to run over, pull Heidi close and soothe her pain. But that probably wouldn't be appreciated or welcomed by this porcupine of a kid. Wonder where she got her quills?

So instead, Phoebe smiled warmly, determined to set an example and, first and foremost, make Heidi feel comfortable and welcome. "Hey, Heidi. Good to see you."

Heidi lifted one narrow shoulder. "Hey."

The greeting lacked enthusiasm, but was civil, and was better than the almost silent treatment and eye rolls Heidi had given her the past two days. "Why don't you put your backpack down behind the counter, and you can help me move the tables and chairs back."

Heidi trudged over and dropped her backpack behind the counter, then stood there and gave Phoebe a dispassionate look. "They look fine the way they are," she stated. "Why are you moving them all over the place?"

"Actually, I already rearranged, but I like them better the old way."

"Really?" Heidi considered the new arrangement. "I think this looks way better."

Phoebe frowned. "How so?"

"Well, this way the aisle leads right in from the door. The flow is better."

"Hmm." Phoebe tilted her head to the side, considering the angled tables and chairs from another perspective. "I hadn't considered the flow."

"Oh, yeah," Heidi said, walking over to the doorway. "See?" She gestured with her hands. "No one has to walk around a table to get to the counter this way."

Heidi was right. But…the tables had been set up the same way for as long as Phoebe could remember. "True. But don't you think they're lopsided this way?" Phoebe asked, canting her head to the side.

"No, they're actually perfectly balanced with three rows on the right and three rows on the left." Heidi pointed. "One, two, three. One, two, three."

"True, true," Phoebe replied, then bit her lip. "I don't know…"

"What's the big deal? They're only tables and chairs." Heidi scrunched her face. "Why don't you try it this way and see how it goes? You can always move them back later."

Phoebe laughed, the sound somewhere between a squeak and a chuckle. "I suppose you're right. So, we'll leave them, and I can always change them back tomorrow." Or tonight after the store closed. Yeah, that made her feel better.

"Great," Heidi said.

Without thought, Phoebe went over and started moving the napkin dispensers on each table so their angles matched those of the tables they sat on.

"What are you doing?" Heidi asked.

"Straightening the napkin holders."

"Why?"

"Um…because I like them that way?"

Heidi's blue eyes blinked. "You actually think about that kind of stuff?"

"Well…yeah. I do." Phoebe continued straightening until all the napkin holders matched. "Customers appreciate a clean, well-organized store."

"Sounds freaky to me," Heidi said. "Has anyone ever actually told you they like the way your napkin-holder things are arranged?"

"No."

Heidi gave her a drop-chinned stare.

"But *I* like them in order."

"Sounds to me like you hate change," Heidi said, plopping into one of the chairs. "I had a friend in Seattle who didn't want anything to be different. She's been wearing the same brand of jeans forever, since she was, like, eight or something."

Phoebe's palms grew damp and she shook her head. "I'm okay with change."

"What kind of shampoo do you use?" Heidi asked out of the blue.

The unexpected question took Phoebe off guard. "Um…Curly Suds," she said with a frown.

"And how long have you been using that shampoo?"

Phoebe thought, then remembered how she'd begged her mom to buy Curly Suds—*Perfect Your Curls with Curly Suds,* the commercial had touted—when it had come out when she was about thirteen or fourteen. She'd been in desperate need of curl perfection, having been called Poodle Head by Jimmy Salton in fifth grade.

She'd been using the shampoo ever since—no more Poodle Head, thank you very much—and she'd actually panicked a few years ago when she'd heard the company was going to stop making the product. Thankfully, that rumor had proven untrue, and a hair disaster of monumental proportions had been averted.

"Since I was a teenager," she replied.

Heidi pointed at her. "See? I told you," she said, her voice victorious. "You hate change. You've probably eaten the same thing for breakfast forever, too, haven't you?"

Phoebe swallowed the small, hard lump in her throat, recalling how Justin had been the first one to make her an open-faced peanut butter and banana on an English muffin when they'd met in college. She'd eaten one every day since and made it a point never to run out of the ingredients. "Not forever, actually," she argued.

"But for a long time, right?"

Phoebe nodded. "Right."

"Told you."

"How did you know?" Phoebe asked.

Heidi seemed to catch herself before she responded. A shadow moved over her face, and then she said, "I dunno, just a feeling."

"Are you sure it's just a feeling?" Phoebe asked. She could have sworn Heidi had been speaking from personal experience.

Heidi looked down at the table, then began picking at her thumbnail. "I guess," she said, her attention focused on her fingernail.

Heidi's vague response, and the shadow Phoebe had seen, ratcheted up Phoebe's curiosity, and she had a ball of compassion building in her chest. She sensed Heidi was holding a lot in, and that didn't seem healthy for anybody, much less a young girl who'd suffered so many emotional blows. Heidi needed to talk, needed a friend, and as long as the lull in customers continued, now seemed like a good time for Phoebe to offer a shoulder.

But what about a shoulder, or even a sympathetic ear, for Heidi's father? Not so much.

Slowly, Phoebe sat down next to Heidi. "You sound like you knew that I'd eaten the same breakfast because you had personal experience with something like that."

Heidi gave Phoebe a wary look, then shrugged. "So?"

"So, maybe you'd like to talk about it."

"With you?"

"Well, yeah. I'm a good listener, and I'd like to help," Phoebe said, speaking the truth. How could she turn her back on this girl?

"You want to help me?" Heidi asked with a scowl.

"Yes, I would."

"Why?" Heidi said, slamming her blond eyebrows together.

"Why not?"

Heidi went to work on her thumbnail again. "I shoplifted from you, and I've been kinda mean the last few days." Something akin to shame bloomed on her face. "Why would you want to help *me?*"

Phoebe's heart melted. This was a good kid sitting before her, one who'd lost her way and covered up her pain by acting out. All the more reason to offer to help.

Phoebe debated finessing her way through her response, and not sharing with Heidi that she knew about her brother and her mom. But she discarded the idea; Heidi needed honesty and understanding, not smoke and mirrors and seemingly false platitudes. She needed to know that Phoebe truly did empathize.

"Because I know what you've been through, honey, and I know how you feel," Phoebe said quietly.

Heidi froze. "What do you mean?"

"I know about your mom and your brother."

"You do?" Heidi asked in an agony-tinged whisper.

Phoebe nodded.

A long silence. And then fat tears built in Heidi's eyes. "Who told you?"

Unease rippled through Phoebe. "Your dad."

Heidi pressed her lips together, and she blinked several times. "He promised not to tell anyone."

Oh, boy. Why hadn't Carson warned her? Tactical error all around, despite everyone's good intentions.

On the heels of that chagrined thought, another thought rolled sharp wheels through Phoebe's mind.

Did Heidi even know Carson was attending the grief-counseling class?

Either way, it wasn't Phoebe's place to bring it up. That bit of information was strictly between father and daughter.

Phoebe bit her lip, stalling ever so slightly. She'd need to walk quietly here. "He told me in the strictest confidence," she said, trying to smooth over her verbal faux pas.

Heidi's face tightened, even as fat tears rolled down her pale cheeks. "I can't believe he told you."

She reached out and touched Heidi's hand. "It's okay—"

"No, it's not," Heidi said, jumping to her feet. "Nothing is ever going to be okay again."

Her words tore at Phoebe. Phoebe knew the feeling where you thought your life was over and would never be the same. "Honey—"

"Don't call me honey," Heidi said on a sob. "I'm not your honey."

Phoebe stood, her hands clenched at her sides, connecting with all of the emotions pouring out of Heidi. And also understanding the need to choose her words carefully. Heidi was angry, sad; the wrong tactic could be disastrous.

God? I need a little guidance here…

Phoebe hesitated a moment too long, and before she could figure out how to not make things worse, Heidi swiped at her tears and turned and ran for the door, almost crashing into a young mom and dad entering the parlor with a baby in a stroller.

Somehow, she managed to squeeze around the surprised couple and the huge stroller, and in a blur of blond hair—and another heartrending sob—she was gone.

Phoebe took a frantic couple of steps in the direction of the door then slammed on the brakes, not wanting to muscle her way around the couple hovering in the doorway, or knock the baby out of the stroller.

Instead she drew in a hitched breath and tried to calm down. She could fix this. Plastering on a smile, she looked at the customers, already formulating plans to give them their ice cream for free.

"Sorry about that. She didn't see you." She waved them forward, out of the doorway. "Come on in."

They nodded their assent, and entered.

Thankfully, Tanya walked in behind them, back from lunch. Whew. Just in time. Phoebe would try to catch Heidi before she got too far.

Still smiling, she said, "Tanya, would you help these nice people, and give them whatever they want on the house?" She infused an unruffled demeanor she didn't feel into her voice.

Tanya widened her hazel eyes but didn't argue or ask for an explanation. "Be happy to."

"Great." She pressed a hand to Tanya's shoulder, then leaned in and said, "Heidi ran off. I'll be right back." Hopefully.

Her heart pounding, she ran out the door into the

May sunshine, shading her eyes with her hand. She cast her gaze right then left, craning her head to see around the tourists on the boardwalk, hoping Heidi had stopped to calm down.

Nothing. Heidi was nowhere in Phoebe's immediate view. She'd probably darted down a side street or something. Hopefully she'd headed straight home, which was…where? Moonlight Cove, she presumed, and close enough to walk, since Heidi had told Phoebe she'd walked home after the shoplifting incident.

Making a quick decision, Phoebe took off toward the police station two short blocks away. By the time she looked up the phone number and called, she could be at Carson's side.

As Phoebe hustled along the boardwalk, half running, half walking, regret dug sharp talons into her. She'd handled Heidi all wrong, said things she shouldn't have. Made Heidi cry, for goodness' sake! Nice move.

To make matters worse, she had to deliver the news to Carson that she'd upset his daughter so much the child had run out of the parlor sobbing, and Phoebe had no idea where she'd gone.

A sharp sense of dread mixed with worry bolted through Phoebe. She picked up the pace, breaking into an outright run, managing to avoid the shoppers on the boardwalk with some fancy footwork and sheer determination to reach Carson as quickly as possible.

Without thought, another prayer rose from her lips as she neared the station.

Please, Lord, watch over and keep Heidi safe until we can find her.

Because Carson would never forgive her, and she would never forgive herself, if something happened to Heidi.

And no matter what, Phoebe had a sinking feeling he'd be livid she'd foolishly shared with Heidi what Carson had revealed in confidence last night.

How could she have made such a mess of things?

Chapter Seven

"Sheriff, Phoebe Sellers is here to see you."

Carson nearly spilled his coffee when he jerked up from the paperwork on his desk toward his office door to look at Rona, the tall, thin receptionist who'd been manning the phones and front desk around here for almost thirty years.

What was Phoebe doing here in the middle of the day?

His gut rolled, and before he could gather his thoughts and speak past the rock in his throat, Phoebe pushed his office door open wider, made herself skinnier and squeezed around Rona, practically knocking the woman over.

"Carson, sorry to barge in, but Heidi ran off from the shop, and I'm not sure where she went," Phoebe announced, her face etched with worry.

He rose, and so did his concern. "What happened?" he asked, coming around his desk.

"We were…talking, and she got upset…" Phoebe

wrung her hands together and cast a worried gaze at Rona hovering in the doorway.

Carson got the unfortunate drift. "Rona, would you please excuse us?" he politely asked.

Rona pursed her scarlet lips, inclined her head and then, in a swish of her yellow-and-orange-flowered skirt, turned and left, closing the door behind her.

Carson wouldn't be surprised if she didn't already have an ear pressed to the door.

He ignored the upsetting thought and swiped a hand through his hair, as if the action could some-how magically keep his head from exploding with worry. "What's going on?"

Phoebe shook her head. "I messed up."

"Explain."

She took a deep breath, let it out slowly and then said in a measured tone, "We were talking, and she seemed so sad. I know how that feels, so I told her I understood what she's going through and…" Phoebe trailed off, her blue eyes begging for his understanding.

"Keep going," Carson said, impatiently gesturing in the air with his hand. He had a bad feeling he knew where this conversation was headed.

"And…" She bit her lip. "Well, I didn't know what you told me was a secret, and I let it slip that I knew what had happened."

He slammed his eyebrows together.

Phoebe visibly swallowed. "Our conversation last night?" she said, wincing.

"About her mom and her brother?" he bit out.

Phoebe nodded again. "And she started crying, jumped up and ran out."

"Didn't you try to stop her?"

"Of course I did. But there were customers in the doorway, and by the time I got outside, she was gone."

He automatically went into cop mode and pulled out his cell phone, knowing now wasn't the time to lay into Phoebe for upsetting his daughter. That fun little discussion could wait until he knew Heidi was safe. "How long ago was this?"

"Less than ten minutes."

"Guess it's time to get my kid a cell phone so I can call her every time she takes off. Great." He punched speed dial number one, willing himself to not imagine the worst, which had been a major challenge for him the minute his son had died in front of him. "I'm calling Mrs. Philpot. Hopefully Heidi goes straight home."

As the phone rang on the other end of the line, Carson watched Phoebe pace, her arms crossed over her waist, her shoulders noticeably stiff.

She was obviously sweating the situation, and part of him felt bad that she'd gotten swept up in the ongoing drama of the Winters family.

Yet another part blamed himself for letting down his usual guard by spilling to Phoebe about CJ, and not telling her that he'd promised Heidi he wouldn't tell anyone about CJ. Double whammy. Guess there was a lesson there.

Mrs. Philpot answered after four rings. "Winters residence."

"Mrs. Philpot, this is Carson. Is Heidi there?"

"No, Sheriff, she's working at the ice cream store this afternoon, remember?"

"I know, but she got upset and ran off, and I thought she might have made it home already." Wishful thinking—their house was about a half mile from the center of town, and would take at least fifteen minutes to reach on foot—but hope won out.

"Oh, dear," Mrs. Philpot said, her tone grave. "She hasn't arrived here yet." A pause. "How long ago did she run off?"

"Ten minutes."

"Then she wouldn't be here by now."

"I know. It's possible she didn't even go home." He squeezed the bridge of his nose. "But I don't have anything else to go on, so I'll take a swing through town, then drive home and keep an eye out for her on the way in case she's in transit."

"I'll call you if she shows up here," Mrs. Philpot said.

"Thanks. Let's just hope we figure out where she is by the time I get there."

"Would you like me to call some of her friends?" Mrs. Philpot asked.

"No, let's not get everybody worried just yet. If we don't find her soon, then we'll go to Plan B."

"Okay, Sheriff. I'll keep the phone in my hand and let you know the minute she arrives."

Bless the woman for being so levelheaded. "Thank you," he said, and then pressed End.

The phone had barely cut off before Phoebe said from behind him, "I'm going with you."

He looked at the floor to slow his heart, then up at Phoebe, noting the determined set to her chin and her level, just-try-to-stop-me stare. Part of him admired her for her resolve. Part of him wanted to put her in a rowboat in the middle of Moonlight Cove Lake and keep the oars.

He didn't have time for either reaction, and he had a feeling trying to stop her would be a waste of precious time.

"Fine." He grabbed his hat from the coatrack by the door on his way out. "I don't have time to argue."

To her credit, she didn't thank him or try to give him her opinion, and he was sure she had one. She simply hustled into step behind him and stayed silent as he headed out to his cruiser in the parking lot behind the station. He hollered to Rona on his way that he was leaving.

Carson welcomed Phoebe's silence now—he didn't need any distractions from finding Heidi. But sooner or later, he and Phoebe would have a very frank discussion about what had happened at the ice cream parlor with her and Heidi.

He jammed his hat onto his head.

And that wasn't a conversation he was looking forward to having.

The silence in the police truck was deafening.

Phoebe told herself this was to be expected as she slanted a glance over at Carson and saw the little muscle tick in his jaw again.

With spare efficiency he negotiated the car up Main Street and out of the south end of town, his large hands tight on the steering wheel of his SUV. As he drove, his laserlike gaze swept left and right beneath the brim of his hat for any sign of Heidi.

Per his terse instructions when they'd left the police station, Phoebe also kept her eyes peeled for Heidi. Hopefully the girl was on her way home and they'd see her and that would be that. No harm, no foul.

But what if they didn't find her? What if something unthinkable happened? The thought made Phoebe literally ill.

She clenched her hands in her lap and bit her tongue, resisting the strong urge to explain to Carson what had happened with her and Heidi in greater detail. To make him understand Phoebe had had the best of intentions.

Now, though, was not the time to expect a discussion.

She sent up a silent prayer to God for Heidi's safety, then sat quietly and scanned the passing sidewalks. Nothing. Where had Heidi gone?

About a half mile outside of the main part of town,

Carson turned into an older development called Cove Shores. The houses here were mostly mid-fifties ramblers with large lots, and while the majority were relatively well kept, some had fallen into clear disrepair and had overgrown yards and peeling paint. A few even had junker cars languishing in the moss-covered driveways.

She was a bit surprised he lived here, given there were much nicer, newer neighborhoods just across the highway. But there were a lot of rentals in this neighborhood. Maybe he was renting until he found something nicer?

He hung a quick right onto Gull Court, and then, after driving about three blocks, made a sweeping left turn and brought the SUV to a lurching halt in the driveway of a midcentury ranch badly in need of a coat of paint.

While the yard wasn't overgrown, it was dull and sparse, and had little formal landscaping to speak of. A patch of scraggly, lifeless grass covered the small front yard. The flower beds had probably sported annuals at one time, but now they were nothing but dirt. The place had a sad, neglected feel to it that made Phoebe's heart hurt.

Ignoring the sensation as best she could, she noted the newer blue compact car they'd pulled next to in the driveway. And the older flame-haired woman dressed in a lime-green sweatsuit hovering on the porch, her arms crossed over her chest.

Undoubtedly Mrs. Philpot.

Carson punched a button and rolled down his window as the babysitter came hurrying forward, shaking her head.

"She's not here yet, Sheriff," she said, drawing up to Carson's window, her brow furrowed.

Carson whacked his hand on the steering wheel. The sound tore through Phoebe like a knife.

"Would you like me to get in my car and help you look?" Mrs. Philpot asked.

He rubbed his shadowed jaw. "No, I need you to stay here in case she shows up."

Mrs. Philpot nodded her agreement.

Phoebe leaned forward. "Maybe we should go drive around town and look some more."

Just then, his radio went off. He jammed a rigid finger into a button on the dash and said, "Yes, Rona?"

Rona's voice crackled across the radio. "We just got a call from Molly Kent. Apparently your daughter is at Bow Wow Boutique, and Molly thought you'd want to know."

A tide of relief swept through Phoebe, and judging by the sudden sag to Carson's broad shoulders, he was feeling the same sense of reprieve.

"Thanks, Rona," he said. "Let Molly know I'll be right there."

"Sure thing, Chief. Over and out."

"Over and out," Carson repeated.

Mrs. Philpot pressed a hand to her chest. "Oh, thank goodness she's okay."

"Amen," Carson muttered, his hands now slack on

the steering wheel. After a moment, he looked at Mrs. Philpot. "I'll go get her and bring her home."

Phoebe read his subtext—Heidi wouldn't be coming back to the parlor today. *Or maybe...ever?*

"Of course, Sheriff," Mrs. Philpot replied, backing up a step. "I'll be waiting for her."

Carson tipped his head. "That would be great, Mrs. P. You're a gem. Thank you."

"You're welcome, Sheriff," she said, then leaned down and looked at Phoebe through the window. "I'm Carolyn Philpot, by the way."

"I figured that," Phoebe said. "Phoebe Sellers."

"Sorry we're not meeting under more relaxed circumstances."

"Me, too," Phoebe replied.

Mrs. Philpot headed up the driveway.

His jaw still resembling granite, Carson shifted the SUV into Reverse, backed up into the street and shoved the gearshift into Drive. He gunned the engine and the vehicle jumped forward, headed in the direction they'd just come from.

Phoebe sat next to him, worrying a hangnail on her thumb, her throat tight. She was definitely on his list, as was painfully evident when his conversational skills didn't improve as they returned to town.

And to a reckoning Phoebe wasn't sure she wanted to face.

As Carson drove from his house into the main part of town, his shoulders gravitated away from his ears, and the harsh voice of worry that had been jabbing at him since Phoebe had shown up at the station thankfully shut up.

Crisis averted. Daughter safe. Status: apparently fine.

He stopped at the light at Tenth and Main and glanced quickly at Phoebe without turning, noting her knotted hands in her lap and overall stiff posture. Her tense silence seemed as big as the gigantic land mammal figuratively sharing the vehicle.

They needed to talk.

Heidi was out of harm's way, so he allowed himself to de-compartmentalize his thoughts and focus his energy directly on thinking about what he was going to say to Phoebe.

Now that he'd had a bit of time to calm down, he realized that he should have been up-front with Phoebe about his promise to Heidi not to divulge details of their personal life to anyone. He really couldn't blame Phoebe for talking to his daughter about CJ and Susan. Phoebe wasn't a mind reader. He owed her an apology.

"I'm going to go park by Molly's place," he said as he hit the Moonlight Cove main drag.

"Okay," Phoebe answered, her voice small.

The forlorn tone of her voice made something inside of him shift. He stopped at another light, and, unable to help himself, he turned and looked at her.

She turned his way and gave him a tremulous smile, obviously trying to put on a brave face. But her eyes glittered with tears. "Carson, I'm so sorry." She sniffed. "I…I want you to know that I only had good intentions, and I didn't know I wasn't supposed to say anything."

"I know. It's my fault, and I apologize for being curt. Don't worry, all right?"

Phoebe nodded, blinking. "All right."

He opened his door and climbed out, adjusting his utility belt as he straightened. Nodding to Bertram Loud, the local bank manager who was so old and crippled he could barely shuffle along the boardwalk unassisted—how the man still worked every day was beyond Carson—he turned in the direction of Molly's store.

Phoebe fell in beside him. "Um…is it okay if I come with you?"

He stopped and put his hands on his hips. "I'm not sure that would be a good idea," he replied, thinking of Heidi.

Wordlessly, Phoebe nodded. She cast her eyes down, then, seeming to think better of backing off, she looked up and came forward half a step, her hand outstretched. With her eyes radiating pure blue sincerity, she said in a rushed tone, "Would you reconsider? I really want to make sure she's okay, and I'd like to apologize."

He stared at her, chewing on his cheek.

"I'll only stay a minute," Phoebe said before he could respond, her voice laced in a winning tone clearly meant to convince him to let her go with him.

Her tactic worked. Hoping he didn't regret his decision, he dipped his head. "Fine. But make it quick. I don't want to upset Heidi any more than she already is."

Phoebe's face softened in relief, and her mouth split into a grateful smile that did funny things to his insides. "Thank you. I will. Make it quick, that is."

He turned and headed down the boardwalk and Phoebe fell in beside him, walking quickly to keep up with his long stride. He was anxious to see Heidi.

As he drew up to Bow Wow Boutique, the wind coming off the ocean a block away tugged on the brim of his hat and brought the scent of salt and rain. The forecast called for rain by nightfall, continuing on for the next few days.

Grimly, he set his jaw, readying himself to have a heart-to-heart with Heidi. One where he ate crow and explained why he'd betrayed her confidence.

Unfortunately, the weather front moving in wasn't the only nasty storm brewing. Not by a long shot.

Chapter Eight

Her heart in her throat, Phoebe stepped into Bow Wow Boutique, Carson an unmistakable presence behind her. She was thankful he'd capitulated and let her hang around to speak with Heidi. Phoebe's conscience demanded she apologize and then fix her blunder and assure Heidi that she was a friend and not an enemy. If that was possible.

Before the door had closed behind them, Molly rushed forward. "She's fine."

Carson cast his gaze around. "Where is she?"

"In my office playing with Peter and Parker."

Carson raised his brows in question.

"My miniature schnauzers," Molly explained. "I'm a big Spider-Man fan." Molly's copper brows slammed together as her gaze caught on Phoebe. "Why do you look like you need a hug?"

Before Phoebe could react, Molly stepped forward and gave her a quick, heartfelt hug only a longtime friend could offer. Phoebe's tension eased a teensy bit.

Carson cleared his throat. "What happened?"

"She showed up here, crying, upset," Molly said, moving behind the checkout counter. "The dogs greeted her, and they seemed to calm her down. So I suggested they go play in my office, and then I remembered that Phoebe had said when we talked earlier today that Heidi was working at her store this afternoon, so I called Phoebe to see what was up."

"Go on," Carson prompted.

"So," Molly said. "Tanya answered the phone at the parlor and told me Phoebe had taken off to find Heidi, so I called the station and talked to Rona and told her what was up. She said you two had left together, and she then called you. I encouraged Heidi to stay until you got here."

Made sense. "Heidi must have come in here right after she left my store," Phoebe said. "She wasn't on the boardwalk when I checked right after she ran out."

"She seemed embarrassed to be crying. I got the sense she was hiding," Molly said.

Phoebe lifted her shoulders. "That would be my fault."

"Say what?" Molly said, pulling in her chin.

Carson cut in. "I'm going to go talk to Heidi." He pointed toward the back of the store. "I assume your office is back there?"

Molly nodded.

"Thanks," he said, already in motion.

Phoebe watched him walk back to Molly's office. He hesitated for a moment by the door and seemed to be bracing himself. Funny how the big, brave cop could be brought low by a twelve-year-old girl. Although, from what she'd seen, the title of Dad was way more daunting than that of Sheriff.

She didn't envy him his position.

After a moment, he quietly opened the door and disappeared inside the office, closing the door behind him.

Call her silly, but Phoebe had an odd urge to be a fly on the wall in that office; the dynamic between father and daughter fascinated her.

And that, in turn, had anxiety eating away at her. Why was she getting so caught up in a situation that was, essentially, none of her business, and potentially dangerous emotionally?

"What's going on with you and the sheriff?" Molly said, drawing Phoebe's attention away from her unwanted reaction to the Winterses' family drama unfolding before her like an Afterschool Special.

Trust Molly to cut to the heart of the matter.

Phoebe released a large breath. "Heidi arrived at the store, and we started talking. One thing led to another, and I said something about—" She cut herself off just in time; the last thing she should do was share information about Carson's son with Molly. She'd learned her lesson about running off at the mouth regarding *that* subject. Very well.

"About what?" Molly prompted.

Phoebe bit her lip. "I can't say."

A thoughtful pause. "Okay," Molly replied, nodding. "Care to tell me why?"

"Carson shared some…things with me last night—"

"You were with Carson last night?"

Phoebe gave herself a mental head slap. She absolutely did not want to awaken the ruthless Matchmaker Molly with talk of spending time with Carson. But she wasn't going to lie, either. She'd tell the truth, and hope Molly dropped the subject. Not likely, knowing Molly, but what other option did Phoebe have?

"Um…yes?" Phoebe said.

"On a *date?*" Molly asked, her voice rising an octave.

"No, no." Phoebe laughed, trying to sound relaxed when she was anything but after the day's stressful events. "Don't get excited, Moll. We weren't on a date." Phoebe didn't date. Anyone. Right?

"But you were with him last night, talking…?" Molly said, her eyes ablaze with interest. So much for dropping the subject. Suddenly, the proverbial lightbulb went on. "Hey, didn't you have grief-counseling last night?"

After having messed up by saying too much to Heidi, Phoebe was going to be extra careful now; Carson might not want her spreading around that he was in a grief-counseling class. "We went to have coffee, and that's all I can say."

Without missing a beat, Molly said, "This is big." She pressed her mouth into a smile.

Here we go again. "No, no, it's not," Phoebe said,

holding up her hands. "It was just coffee, and I can't give any more details." True enough.

Molly's smile grew bigger, and her green eyes sparkled with excitement. "Okay."

Tapping a finger on the counter, Phoebe sighed. "Look, Moll, you've got to let this go. There's nothing going on between me and the sheriff." To protect her heart, Phoebe would make sure of it.

"You showed up with him here today." Molly gestured with her chin to Phoebe's office. "You've clearly bonded with Heidi."

"I haven't spent enough time with her to bond." Heidi wasn't exactly the easiest kid to get to know. Although, something about Heidi touched Phoebe in a way she'd never really experienced. Their shared grief, more than likely. "And I'm only here now because I went with him to look for Heidi, and then insisted on apologizing."

"Still…I sense there's more going on here than just coffee."

"No, there's not."

"I know you, Phoebs," Molly said.

True. "And?" Phoebe asked, almost afraid to hear what her remarkably intuitive friend had to say.

"And to me, it's obvious from the look in your eyes and from your actions that you're getting sucked into the Winters family in a big way."

Phoebe opened her mouth to deny that loaded statement and literally couldn't speak.

Molly had no such problem. "C'mon, Phoebe, why lie to yourself?" she asked.

Flummoxed, Phoebe looked at Molly, a question in her eyes.

Molly reached out and laid a comforting hand on Phoebe's forearm. "Don't you think you should be honest and admit that you're pretty tangled up with the sheriff and his daughter?"

Molly's words rang true. So why on earth was Phoebe having so much trouble staying on the safe, familiar path?

"Maybe you should just go with the flow and see where your feelings about Carson lead."

Phoebe swallowed. "I'm not sure I can go there. Just the thought of letting down my guard with Carson scares me to death."

"I know it's scary," Molly said. "I felt the same way about admitting my feelings for Grant."

All Phoebe could do was nod weakly. Molly had fought falling for Grant tooth and nail, but true love had prevailed in the end.

Molly had her happily ever after.

But Phoebe firmly believed a happily ever after wasn't in her future. So thinking about going with the flow with Carson as Molly had suggested was about as likely as sprouting wings and flying south for the winter.

The bells on the shop's door rang, signaling the arrival of a customer. Molly looked toward the door, then came around the counter. "So, what are you going to do about the situation?" she asked as she walked by Phoebe toward the front of the store where a tall, gray-haired woman browsed the leash display.

"Good question," Phoebe replied. One she'd have to answer sooner or later.

She glanced toward the closed office door, imagining the handsome, enigmatic man behind it.

Yeah. She chose later.

Carson sat in Molly's desk chair, frustration bubbling through him as he watched Heidi flopped out on the giant dog bed in the corner of the office, both dogs vying for the best spot in her lap.

Ignoring him, she showered hugs and kisses on Peter and Parker, who had obviously decided that she was the best thing in the world since the invention of canned dog food.

He bit back a snort. Even *dogs* rated higher than he did right now. Great.

He'd been back here with Heidi for ten minutes, and the only words she'd said were, "How could you?" Her voice had broken into a sob as she'd spoken, and fresh tears had brimmed and run down her rosy cheeks.

Obviously, she thought he'd betrayed her.

Talk about a knife to the heart. The serrated, cut-both-ways kind.

He rubbed his jaw. Guess there was no help for what he had to do—level with her about the grief counseling so he could explain why he'd told Phoebe about CJ and Susan.

He'd planned on telling Heidi that he was attending the classes in time, after he had a better chance to come to terms with his decision to actually confront and deal with his grief. With today's crisis, that strategy was down the tube. Time for the contingency plan he'd hastily thrown together two minutes ago, when it had been obvious she wasn't talking. Or forgiving.

He leaned forward, resting his forearms on his thighs. "Honey, I understand why you're mad at me for talking to Ms. Sellers about CJ and your mom."

Heidi didn't say anything to that. Instead, she buried her head in Peter's—or was it Parker's?—furry silver head.

The animal turned and looked at him with big black eyes. Was the dog gloating?

"Fine, I understand why you don't want to talk. So just listen," he told her.

The other dog nudged her hand and snuggled under her arm.

At her meaningful silence, he cleared his throat and continued. "I normally wouldn't have said anything to Ms. Sellers about what's happened to us. But…I attended a class at the church, and Ms. Sellers was assigned as my partner, so I decided it would be okay to confide in her."

Heidi looked at him sideways through fur, her blue eyes frosty and wary. "What kind of class?" she mumbled into the dog's head.

Though he was grateful for the small victory of getting her to actually talk, he wasn't keen on sharing details about the class; he didn't like admitting he needed help, especially to his daughter. Okay, to anyone.

What other choice was there, though? Heidi needed his honesty, no matter how much it rankled to admit his weakness. So he'd set his misgivings aside and lay it all out there.

This healing process was as much about her as it was him. More about her in his mind, actually. He'd do anything for his daughter.

Clearing his throat again, he said, "A…grief-counseling class."

She froze, then lifted her head to stare at him. "They have those?"

"Yep, they do."

"And Phoebe…um, Ms. Sellers, is in your class?"

He nodded.

Heidi's nose crinkled. "Why does she need help with grief?"

Carson grimaced, belatedly realizing the ramifications of sharing the details of his class with Heidi. Without meaning to, he'd essentially outed Phoebe as having a grief issue.

Nice work.

He looked at the ceiling, suddenly understanding just how Phoebe might have inadvertently let slip to Heidi what Carson had shared with Phoebe about their recent family crises.

He was glad he'd apologized to Phoebe. Hmm. Two in one day. That had to be some kind of personal record.

When he hesitated, Heidi tilted her head to the side. "Did someone she loved die?" she asked in a very small voice.

His breathing backed up. "Honey, that's not my story to tell, so you'll have to ask her to explain." He had a feeling that someone as kind as Phoebe wouldn't mind talking to Heidi about losing her fiancé. Especially if she felt it would help Heidi deal with her loss. But that was Phoebe's call.

Heidi wiped at the drying tears on her face. "Okay."

Thankful to have dodged that bullet, and to have his daughter talking, he extended his hand, hoping Heidi would take it.

To his relief, she did, and his heart started to recover from its funk. He squeezed her small hand in his. "I told Phoebe about CJ and your mom because I truly believed it would help me to handle how…sad I am." The words burned, but he shoved them out anyway, determined to do whatever it took, confront anything, to help Heidi.

Heidi chewed on her lip, then turned red-rimmed eyes up to him. "I'm sad, too, Dad." She sucked in a shaky breath. "I miss Mom and CJ."

Her words got that serrated knife going again. "I know, honey." He swallowed, then tugged on her hand. Thankfully, she didn't resist and came into his arms, a bundle of long, wind-scented hair all mixed up with the light smell of the strawberry lip gloss she wore.

"We both lost someone very important, didn't we?" he said in her ear. Two someones, actually. Times two.

Mother. Brother. Wife. Son. Heidi's whole world had fallen apart. He made a mental note to talk to Lily again about finding a counselor for Heidi.

She tightened her arms around him and nodded against his neck, then sniffed.

"I need you to talk to me about how you're feeling, okay?" He was beginning to understand how important it was for them to talk, communicate. Not his strong suit—the exact opposite, actually—but obviously things had to change. He was going to have to dig deep.

"Okay." She pulled back and looked at him, her blue eyes solemn. "Talking is good, right?"

"Right." New territory for him, yes, this emotional sharing. And truthfully, he didn't like looking his flaws in the eye—never had. But for Heidi…surely he could find a way to open up a bit.

"Can we talk now?"

"Sure."

"Why did Mom leave?" she whispered.

His chest caved in. It was time for the conversation he'd been dreading since the day Susan had walked out, just like that, while Heidi was at school. Shamefully, he'd avoided anything but a vague explanation to Heidi about Susan's desertion; how did a dad explain to his daughter why her mom took off without a word, and hadn't been back? Worse, how could he admit that his own failure to protect CJ had caused Heidi's mom to leave in the first place?

Susan blamed him for their son's death, and would

never forgive him. Her words, not his, which made sharing the truth with Heidi that much harder.

His own guilt bit hard as the truth of Susan's stance slashed into him all over again. Her need to blame had overridden their love—smashed it, really—and that reality was just as hard to accept now as it had been the day she'd walked out, leaving his heart in shreds, his daughter inconsolable for weeks and him without a clue how to fix it all.

But this was about Heidi, not his reactions to Susan's actions, and he did his best to ignore the hard-edged emotions Susan's desertion had caused so he could answer his daughter's questions. Again, it was all about her now; he'd deal with Susan's betrayal as best he could without dragging Heidi through the muck of the dynamic that had played out between him and his ex-wife and had torn their family apart.

"Honey, you know how I told you how upset your mom was when CJ died?" he said, repeating the words he'd come up with late one night a few months ago. He'd known this conversation was inevitable. Shame on him for putting it off.

"Uh-huh. She was crying all the time, and you guys fought a lot."

All true, to his regret. In the wake of CJ's death and the bitter, agonizing grief that followed, both he and Susan had made some bad parenting choices and hadn't shielded Heidi from their heated arguments as well as they should have.

"Well, your mom was still sad, and her sadness

wasn't going away. So…she decided that she needed to get away instead."

Heidi nodded. "So she didn't want to be sad around us?"

"Exactly," he said, treading a very fine line to make this discussion less traumatic for Heidi—if there was such a thing, which he doubted. Even so, he'd do his best to soothe Heidi's hurt.

Would his best be good enough, though?

Heidi turned innocent blue eyes up to him. "Didn't she know we'd help her not be sad?"

Heidi's words struck a harmonious chord, and he instantly knew her guileless statement held a very profound truth he needed to embrace. "I…guess she didn't realize that," he said, amazed at how much wisdom was stored up inside Heidi. Wisdom he needed to heed if they were going to rebound from the losses they'd suffered.

"I wish I could have told her," Heidi said. "She probably would have felt a lot better if she'd known I'd help her."

He squeezed her chin.. "You're probably right. And that's why I want you to always talk to me about how you're feeing, all right?" He'd do his best to do the same, even if it killed him.

"Okay, I promise," she said. Then she tipped her head to the side and furrowed her brow. "So if talking is good, then it's great that you and Ms. Sellers are talking partners, don't you think?" Heidi asked, all innocent honesty.

He blinked. Except they weren't partners anymore, were they? He'd cut out on Phoebe last night the minute the going had gotten tough. "Um…yes," he replied, thrown for a loop by Heidi's perceptiveness, and by her statement, too. Although, given her wise words about the benefits of discussion, he shouldn't be too surprised by her question. Maybe he'd have to reconsider his decision to back out of being partners with Phoebe…

"Oh, good," Heidi said. "She's nice, and she has grief and so do you. Sounds like she would be a good friend."

"I hadn't thought of that," he said, infusing an evenness into his voice that he sure didn't feel.

Heidi laid her cool hand on his cheek. "That's why you have me, Dad."

He gave her a questioning look.

She pursed her lips. "I think of things you don't, silly."

"Yes, you do." He hugged her tight, thankful to have her where she belonged, but not sure how he felt about her forcing him to look beneath the surface of his relationship with Phoebe. "I don't know what I would do without you."

"Me, neither," she said, giving him a smile that lit up his heart.

One of the dogs barked, and Heidi jumped out of Carson's arms. "Okay, Parker, okay." She bent down and patted his head. "You are so spoiled!"

The dog held his chin up for a scratch, and Heidi

obliged. The other one—Peter—nosed his way in and got some of the attention. One of them let out a doggy groan of pure happiness. Guess when you were a dog, a good chin scratching was just about canine bliss.

Heidi giggled. "You want some, too, don'tcha, Peter?"

Peter yipped and then tried to shove Parker out of the way to claim all the good stuff for himself.

Carson looked down at his daughter, glad she was feeling better. Talking had helped, thank goodness. He had to take their discussion one step further, though, and impress upon her that she couldn't go temporarily missing every time she got distraught. He knew too well how dangerous and unpredictable the world could be. Even in a small town, bad things could happen to an unsupervised kid. Look at what had happened to CJ, right under Carson's nose…

With his protectiveness spurring him on, he said, "Heidi, honey, you have to promise me not to run off like you did ever again. You scared me and Ms. Sellers a lot, and Mrs. P., too."

Heidi looked up, blinking, her mouth pressed down at the corners.

He went on. "In fact, Ms. Sellers was so worried, she came here with me to get you."

"I'm sorry," Heidi said, looking sheepish. "I didn't mean to scare you guys."

"I know, and I accept your apology." He could see she was truly remorseful. "But from now on when you're upset, don't run away. Talk to me, all right?"

She nodded. "Can I talk to Ms. Sellers, too, if she says it's all right? I guess I need to apologize."

"Sure," he shoved out, his voice higher than normal; was it wise to encourage a relationship between his daughter and Phoebe? But, what else was he going to say? No? He ought to be glad Heidi had found someone in Moonlight Cove she connected with.

"Great." Heidi sprang up, and the dogs followed suit, their stubby tails wagging, their black eyes trained on her. "Let's go talk to her now."

She darted past him and opened the door, heading out to the main part of the store. The dogs followed, obviously thrilled to have a human playmate to chase.

Carson hung back, his stomach dropping like a rock.

Looked as if Heidi was already getting attached to Phoebe. Good for Heidi.

But for him? He wasn't so sure.

Chapter Nine

The door to the office opened, and Phoebe saw Heidi emerge, followed by Peter and Parker dashing at her heels. Though her cheeks were still red and her eyes swollen, she had thankfully stopped crying.

"I'll call the dogs," Molly said, moving sideways as she picked up a package of their favorite—and smelliest—treats. "Peter? Parker? Come." She rustled the bag of treats as extra incentive for the food-driven canines to actually obey.

The dogs skittered on the dog-friendly linoleum and changed course almost in midstride. With twin yips they ran over to Molly, clearly sensing a reward, which Molly dutifully handed out after they both skidded to a stop and sat in front of her.

Phoebe darted a look back to the open office door, and a moment later Carson came out, his expression inscrutable as he replaced his hat on his head. Maybe she was imagining it, but it seemed as if some of the worry lines around his mouth and eyes had smoothed just a bit since they'd arrived, hot on Heidi's trail.

Had he and Heidi worked things out?

Phoebe hoped so; she'd feel awful if her slipup had caused any kind of lasting rift between father and daughter.

Heidi walked over to where Phoebe stood by the front counter. On her way, the girl's face took on a serious, slightly hangdog cast.

Phoebe did her best to project understanding; she knew what was coming, and how she'd react—with an apology, and damage control if necessary.

Heidi came right up to her and looked her in the eye. "Ms. Sellers?"

Phoebe gave her a gentle smile. "Why don't you call me Phoebe."

Heidi nodded. "'kay." She took a breath. "Um… Phoebe. I'm sorry I ran off and made you so worried. My dad explained to me back there why he told you about CJ and my mom," Heidi said earnestly.

Phoebe lifted her eyebrows.

"'Cause you're discussion partners," Heidi said.

Not anymore. Phoebe looked at Carson again. He widened his eyes, nodding.

"Er…yes, that's right, we are," Phoebe said, leaving out the past tense per Carson's nonverbal direction, even as she wondered what was going on. Had he changed his mind about being partners?

"So I told him talking is good," Heidi said with a simple authority Phoebe found adorable.

"You did?"

"Yeah." Heidi cleared her throat. "So I was wondering if you and I could talk sometime about…stuff."

Stuff? As in…

Carson stepped forward. "I told Heidi we're *grief*-counseling discussion partners."

"Ah." Made sense, really, that he would share that with Heidi. "I see." But…had he told Heidi about Justin? For some reason, Phoebe hoped he hadn't; she wasn't opposed to Heidi knowing Justin had died, but she wanted to be the one to divulge that information, on her own terms.

"I also told her that your story was yours to tell, if you wanted to," Carson added.

So he'd left out details. Smart man. "Thank you."

"So, could we talk sometime?" Heidi asked again. "Maybe I need a discussion partner, too."

"What about your dad?" Phoebe asked, not wanting to step on any toes after messing up so royally earlier today. "Don't you think you should talk to him about this?"

"Oh, he and I agreed I'll talk to him more," Heidi said. "But…I like you, Ms. Se…um, Phoebe, and you've been really nice to me." She chewed on her lip. "And it sounds like you know what it's like to lose someone." The last few words came out on a whisper.

Phoebe's chest squeezed. Unfortunately, she knew all too well what it was like to suffer the loss of a loved one, what it felt like to have your heart whole one minute and crushed into tiny bits by grief the next.

And she was heartsick the feeling was mutual between her and Heidi.

Given that sad but true reality, how could she refuse Heidi's request?

Unless, of course, Carson didn't approve. He was in the driver's seat regarding Heidi, and after what had happened today with Heidi running off, Phoebe would never step over that borderline again without his express approval.

She turned and regarded him as he stood silently by just a few feet away, listening and watching over his daughter in a Papa Bear way that sent ripples of admiration through Phoebe.

After a pause, he gave her another scant nod of consent. Okay. Looked as if she had his blessing for her and Heidi to be new BFFs.

"Sure, Heidi, I think that would be nice. Maybe we can talk some when you come to work at the parlor tomorrow."

"Great!" Heidi exclaimed, her face alight with a brilliant smile.

Carson stepped forward. "Glad you two worked this out," he said. He turned his attention to his daughter. "Heidi, I have to take you home. Mrs. P. is waiting there for you."

"Okay, Dad. Guess I'll have to apologize to her, won't I?"

Carson touched the back of Heidi's head and nodded. "Yes, you will."

Peter and Parker came running up just then. Parker dropped a ragged stuffed bunny at Heidi's feet, backed up and barked. Peter ran interference and shot down a side aisle, looking over his shoulder.

Heidi chuckled and squatted down to pick up the toy. "You guys are so funny."

Parker barked again.

"Go ahead and play with them, honey," Carson said, gesturing in the direction Peter had run. "I'll be with you in a minute."

Heidi grabbed the toy and threw it down the aisle. Parker took off, and Heidi followed.

When she was out of earshot, he looked at Phoebe and said, "I think we need to talk."

"Are you sure you're okay with this arrangement?" she asked, gesturing between herself and Heidi.

"I'm fine with that," he said. "That's not what I want to talk about."

Her tummy lurched. "What do you want to talk about?"

The bells over the door rang, and as the din of the dogs' greeting echoed through the store, a family of five came in and scattered.

"I'd prefer to talk somewhere more private." He adjusted his hat and regarded her with an unwavering dark brown gaze. "Would it be okay if I stopped by the store after you close?"

"Sure, that'd be fine," she replied, somehow keeping the worry from showing in her voice.

But the anxiety was there, grinding away at her. Carson wanted to talk. *Privately.*

Why did she have a feeling that didn't bode well for her?

It was almost nine before Carson left the station and headed to the parlor. He was tired from a stressful day made longer by having to track Heidi down and then having to stay late getting caught up on paperwork he'd been putting off. Luckily Mrs. Philpot and Heidi had already made plans to go to a movie with her grandkids, so Heidi was in good hands for the night.

The sun hadn't set completely yet, but it was on its way toward the horizon as he ambled along the boardwalk, deliberately slowing down to enjoy the lovely coastal evening and decompress a bit after such a hectic, trying day.

He tipped his hat to some young tourists coming out of an art gallery, finally allowing himself to think about the woman he was on his way to see.

Truth be told, he was very impressed with the way Phoebe had handled Heidi today at Bow Wow Boutique. She'd been patient, kind and clearly concerned for his daughter, which always earned extra points in his rather picky book. No doubt about it, Phoebe possessed a gentle, compassionate way that made his insides do funny things.

He grimaced. Funny things he wasn't sure he liked, actually. He wasn't an idiot, and he knew what he was feeling was attraction. And being attracted to any woman right now set his nerves on edge.

Well, seeing as how Heidi had shown him that he needed Phoebe as a discussion partner—wise girl, his baby, even when she was telling him things he didn't want to face—he had no choice but to deal with his attraction to Phoebe, and gut it out. Or simply ignore it.

Either way, he had to get a handle on the situation. Letting himself head down the messy road that led to putting his heart on the line wasn't in his playbook.

So, he thought as he drew up to the door of the parlor, he'd tell Phoebe they were back on as discussion partners. And hope he didn't regret his decision down the line. And that she hadn't changed her mind about being partners since he'd unceremoniously chickened out last night.

A middle-aged man and a woman came out of the store, cones in hand, just as Carson reached for the door. With a respectful nod of his bald head, the man held the door for him with his free hand, and Carson thanked him as he entered.

Phoebe stood by one of the tables, obviously waiting for the customers to leave. As soon as Carson was in, she hurried forward and turned the sign in the window to Closed before the door even had a chance to shut all the way. Hastily, she locked it.

As she turned, he immediately noticed that her cheeks looked pale, and she had faint shadows under her eyes. Concern detonated, but he held it in check.

Maybe she was just tired. It had been a long day for her, too.

"In a hurry to close?" he asked, teasing.

"Actually, I am," she replied, her voice edged in weariness, and something else he couldn't quite put his finger on. Sadness, maybe? Whatever the case, he sensed something was wrong, especially when she started cranking the mini blinds on the windows closed.

"Long day?" he asked as he removed his hat, going with the obvious.

She silently nodded and walked by him, not meeting his gaze.

He followed her. "I don't mean to be pry, but is there something wrong?"

She stopped with her back turned. "Are you sure you want to talk? We're not technically discussion partners anymore."

He winced, but he took the figurative pain; he deserved the barb. "Listen, about that…"

She didn't turn around, didn't respond. She just put her hand on the counter and dipped her head.

He froze, unsure of what to do; he still wasn't certain she wanted him pressing for details. Then he heard what distinctly sounded like a low sob.

Worry bubbled up again, stronger now. This was too unmistakable to ignore or pass off as her simply being worn-out. So he closed the distance between them and peeked around so he could see her down-turned face.

And was stunned to see tears running down her pale cheeks.

"Hey, now," he said, compassion kicking in. He reached out and touched her arm, encouraging her to turn toward him. "What's wrong?"

She gave in to the gentle pressure and looked at him. Then her face crumbled. "Tomorrow is Justin's birthday, and his dad called earlier tonight to see how I was doing."

It didn't take a detective to figure out who Justin was. Her fiancé. Rather than push, Carson took her by the shoulders and guided her to the nearest table. "Sit."

She complied, her shoulders sagging.

Carson sat down next to her. "You want to talk about it?" he asked again, putting her in control.

She pressed her lips together and nodded slightly, tears leaking out of her eyes.

Her crying made his gut burn. "Talking to people who knew CJ is still a challenge for me," he said, hoping his empathy helped her a bit.

Her eyes softened. "You understand, then, don't you?"

"Unfortunately, yes." He got her grief. Perfectly. They had that in common.

She pressed her free hand to her brow, squeezed his hand, and her shoulders started to shake.

Her anguish tore at him. Acting on instinct, he leaned over and put his arm around her, pulling on her hand. "Come here."

She resisted for a second, and then, with a sob, she leaned in his direction and took ahold of his right shoulder from the back, pressing her damp face to the place between his neck and his left shoulder.

The fresh, light scent of her shampoo washed over him, and he actually felt dizzy. It had been a long time since he'd been this close to a woman.

Seemed like a lifetime. Or three.

He closed his eyes, allowing himself to savor the moment of nearness for a measly yet wonderful second. But then he deliberately redirected his thoughts and focused on their discussion rather than having a woman in his arms; thinking about how good it felt to have Phoebe close wasn't what he should be doing right now. She needed him emotionally, and, surprisingly, he wanted to be there for her. Without distractions, as tempting as those distractions might be.

"Have you seen Justin's father since Justin died?" he asked, unable to keep from pressing his nose into her fragrant hair. Call him weak.

"He calls every so often to check in, but I haven't seen him since the funeral. He was a mess, and I was a mess, and I'm ashamed to say I haven't wanted to see him since." She wiped her cheeks. "It's just too hard."

"Why are you ashamed?" he asked, squeezing her slim shoulder.

"He was almost my father-in-law." She sniffed. "I

should be able to be there for him, and instead, just the thought of seeing him makes me cry."

Empathy streaked through him. "You're human," he said. "And we humans aren't perfect." Although he'd often beat himself to a mental pulp about being a wholly imperfect father to CJ.

"I know. I guess I just expect a lot of myself."

He saw that in her, saw her drive to keep it together when she obviously felt more like letting herself fall apart. He was the same way, always trying to maintain iron control to avoid turmoil.

"It's hard when we don't live up to our own expectations for ourselves, isn't it?" He still hadn't forgiven himself for putting CJ in danger.

She pulled back and looked right at him, her brow furrowed. "You sound like you speak from experience."

Oh, yeah. Heartbreaking experience. His throat burned, and he looked away from her probing gaze. All he could think was that the discussion was veering to a place he couldn't go.

She reached out and touched his cheek. "You can talk to me," she whispered.

His face warmed beneath her touch, and her soft voice pulled at him like the moon pulled at the tide, muddling his thoughts even more. But one thought stood out. "I'm not sure that I can," he said truthfully.

Everything inside of him shouted to shut down this

conversation. Right now. Before he had to confront all of the emotions he'd been hiding away since CJ died.

Unable to think or even breathe with her so close, he slowly lifted his arm from around her and put some distance between them. She let him go and sat back in her chair, watching his every move.

He couldn't meet her gaze. Instead, he eyed the door, desperately wanting to escape the excruciating conversation looming.

After a few silent moments, she leaned her forearms on the table. "I see you eyeing the door. You want to take off, don't you?"

Amazing how well she read him. And a bit scary. Was he that transparent? Or was she just that intuitive? Maybe both. Wordlessly, he nodded, unable to push out a lie.

"I understand, really, I do. As I've said before, opening up is a challenge," she said, straightening the metal napkin dispenser on the table until it was lined up nice and square with the edge.

"Yup," was all he could say. If he spoke, he was afraid he'd lose it. And heading toward that kind of emotionally chaotic place? He wasn't going there, even though Phoebe had him looking in that direction.

"You don't like losing control, do you?" she asked, plucking a napkin from the dispenser and dabbing at her damp eyes.

His stomach churned. "Bad things happen when I do that." As in, his son had died when Carson had lost control of the situation, even though as a cop, he'd been trained to do the exact opposite.

"What do you mean?" she asked, pulling a napkin from the dispenser.

He leveled a stare at her, tightening his jaw. "You're not going to stop pushing, are you?"

"Do you want me to?" she volleyed back with a twist of her lips.

He frowned. "Why do you keep answering my questions with another question?"

"Sorry." She lifted her shoulders and let them fall. "I don't know how else to get you to open up."

He felt his walls go up along with his shoulders. "Guess I'm going for enigmatic," he said flippantly, to diffuse the tension going nuts in him.

"Enigmatic, or clueless?" she asked with a dry-eyed, now steely gaze.

"Ouch," he said with an exaggerated cringe. "Zinger."

"Sorry to be blunt."

"Hey, I can take it." He couldn't remember the last time someone had challenged him like this.

"You seem to bring that out in me."

He raised a rigid finger. "Nice excuse, but have you considered that maybe your bluntness is a good way to shift the attention off yourself?" he said, the words sliding out before he could catch them.

For a second, she just sat there, her eyebrows raised in surprise. Then she inclined her head to the side, nodded and said, "Touché."

"So was that really what you were doing?" he asked, surprised she'd admit he'd hit the nail on the head.

"Maybe." She started fiddling with the napkin in her hand. "I've been told I sometimes use blame to... um, deflect."

He laughed without humor. "So I'm a clueless control freak, and you're a blamer slash deflector." He whistled. "What a nice pair we are, huh?" he said facetiously.

"When you put it that way, we do sound kind of sad, don't we?"

"No kidding." He chewed on his cheek, ruminating. "So what should we be learning from this?"

"That maybe being discussion partners is a good thing?" she asked, dipping her chin.

He hated to admit she was right, but he really would be an absolutely clueless idiot instead of a figurative one if he didn't face the truth head-on. "Heidi certainly thinks we should continue talking."

"Well, then, there you have it," Phoebe said, gathering up the napkin she'd shredded. "So are we back on as discussion partners?"

He looked at her unflinching blue gaze, wanting to rise to the challenge she presented. If she could open up, so could he. For Heidi.

"I guess we are," he replied, spreading his hands wide, acting relaxed about their decision.

"Okay, then. That decides it," she said with a businesslike bob of her head. "Glad we worked that out."

"Would you mind if we waited until another time to bleed, though?" He rolled a shoulder. "I'm exhausted." Not to mention he needed time to gut up. Ha. Sounded as if he was facing a firing squad rather than a pretty blonde discussion partner.

"Me, too," she replied, rising. She rubbed her temples. "Nothing like an old-fashioned crying jag to make me feel like a worn-out blob."

He stood. "Trust me, you don't look like a blob." Far from it, unfortunately. She always looked great. "So when do you want to get together again, and where?" Funny how that sounded like they were planning a date—

He jerked his mind away from that loaded thought and managed to stay all casual-looking.

"Can we play that by ear?" Phoebe asked. "With the good weather, the store's going to be busy this weekend, and I'm thinking you're going to be busy with dumb tourist tricks."

"Good point." He grabbed his hat and put it on, thankful for the reprieve. He was game to open up, but needed time to adjust to the firing squ...um, idea. "Just let me know what works for you, all right?"

"All right."

He headed toward the door. Just as he reached for the lock, she said, "Carson?"

He turned.

Moving closer, she put her hands in her jeans pockets. "Listen, thanks for being so understanding when I lost it. I really needed someone to talk to, and I appreciate the shoulder." With a cocked eyebrow, she nodded toward his left shoulder. "Literally."

He looked down and saw her tearstains on his uniform. Somehow the sight of her tears smudging his shirt made his insides twist. He cleared his throat. "Er...you're welcome."

She said good-night and he left, taking a deep pull of the cool, ocean-scented air as he stepped onto the boardwalk and headed to the station to get his rig.

As he walked, the burning lump of trepidation in his gut remained. And while he accepted that the reaction was an inevitable side effect of the chancy path he'd chosen, he couldn't even come close to ignoring the chunk of fire plaguing him.

Because, truthfully, telling Phoebe he was responsible for CJ's death would be one of the hardest things he'd ever done.

Talk about the challenge of a lifetime.

Chapter Ten

At noon the next day, Heidi showed up at the ice cream parlor right when it opened. Phoebe was happy to note that the surly attitude was gone, and Heidi actually had a smile on her face.

Phoebe put her to work at the cash register, figuring it was more practical work experience than cleaning bathrooms. More fun, too, and Phoebe had a feeling Heidi needed some fun in her life after what she'd gone through lately. Plus, she was good with the customers, and with Tanya taking orders and serving, Phoebe had a chance to get caught up paying some bills in the back between checking on things out front periodically.

Of course, bills weren't the only thing on Phoebe's mind. A certain handsome sheriff occupied much of her thoughts, most especially their conversation last night, and the way he'd made her feel better about talking to Justin's father.

Kudos to him for agreeing to be her discussion

partner. She really admired the way he was facing down his fears.

She only hoped she could handle whatever he told her.

Just as she hoped she could forget how comforting it had felt to have his arms around her. She'd help him navigate through handling his grief—and allow him to do the same for her—until the cows came home. But letting herself want to find contentment in his embrace and solace in his physical closeness? Bad idea.

Feeling better after she came to that conclusion— even though she didn't get all of the bills paid—along about five in the afternoon, she went out front, noticing a lull in business. Keeping in mind her promise to Heidi, she headed over to the cash register, pleased to see her patiently helping a little girl count out her money to pay for some candy.

As soon as they were done and the little girl and her mom had left, Phoebe asked Heidi, "You want to take a break so we can talk?"

Heidi closed the register. "You sure it's okay?"

"I'm okay with it." Phoebe looked to Tanya. "Tanya, you think you can hold the fort down for a half hour or so?"

"Sure thing. It's getting close to dinnertime, so things'll be quiet for an hour or two."

"Great. Thanks." Phoebe's gaze landed on the blue sky and sun shining through the window at the front of the store. "How about we get some fresh air and take a walk on the beach?"

"Okay," Heidi said, her eyes lighting up. "It's such a nice day."

"I have a beautiful spot I want to show you," Phoebe said. "Grab your coat and let's go."

Five minutes later, they stepped onto the beach. There were groups of people scattered about, but the beach was wide and long, and not crowded. Though the sun was shining from a clear blue sky, as usual the wind was blowing, making the actual temperature a bit chilly. Still, it was a pretty day, and sunshine was always welcome in a place that saw its share of gray skies and rain.

Moonlight Cove Jetty stretched out in front of them, a dark finger of jagged rock cutting through the waves and whitecaps.

Phoebe pointed left, in the direction of her special spot. "Let's go that way."

They stuck close to the scrub grass edging the beach as they silently walked. Phoebe corralled her hair with her hand and raised her face to the sun, breathing in the fresh ocean air. She savored her time outdoors after working inside all day. Heidi walked silently beside her, noticeably quiet. Was she thinking about the conversation to come?

Phoebe sure was. She had no doubt Heidi was going to ask her about why Phoebe needed grief counseling. Though it was difficult for her to talk about losing Justin, she would talk, for herself, and for Heidi. And Carson for that matter. Interesting how opening up about her loss had become about more than simply helping herself, wasn't it?

Phoebe looked for the large pine tree shaped like a lamb that served as her landmark on the edge of the beach. She headed in that direction, and sure enough, within a minute or so she spotted the large, flat rock she'd found while playing on the beach when she was a kid. She had faithfully returned here to think and clear her mind ever since.

"Let's sit here," she said, gesturing to the rock. "This is my favorite spot."

"Really?"

"Yep. I used to come here all the time when I was your age."

"Cool."

They sat, and for a while, said nothing. Heidi's gaze was focused on the ocean breaking on the shore fifty yards away. Phoebe saw a man and his young son flying a kite a ways down the beach. The man squatted down behind the child, steadying the string as the long, brightly colored kite dipped and whirled in the wind. The sound of the child's happy giggles carried to her on the breeze.

The sight brought to mind thoughts of another father and son, and a pang of grief for Carson moved through her so quickly, so painfully, she actually winced. Her eyes burned, and it had nothing to do with the stiff, salty breeze blowing over her face.

"Are you sad?" Heidi asked.

Phoebe turned, surprised to see Heidi staring at her

with eyes almost the exact color of the cloudless expanse of sky at her back.

She wasn't going to mince words with Heidi; she needed honesty along with compassion. "Actually, I am."

Heidi's gaze followed Phoebe's. After a long silence, she said, "You're thinking about my dad and brother, aren't you?"

Phoebe nodded, not trusting herself to speak.

"Did you lose someone, too?" Heidi asked, her voice whispery soft.

Here came the hard, but necessary, part. Phoebe sucked in a big breath. "Yes, I did."

"Who?"

"My fiancé."

Heidi's mouth formed a small O. "What happened?"

"He was a firefighter, and he got caught in a wildfire and died." And so had her heart.

Until now. The realization sent shockwaves through Phoebe. Definitely something to think about. *Later.*

"Oh. That's sad." Heidi looked down and scuffed her foot on the sand. "I'm sorry."

"Thank you."

"So…um, you know how I feel." A pause. "About CJ dying and my mom leaving?" Heidi's bottom lip quivered.

Phoebe reached out and took Heidi's hand. "Only *you* know your feelings, but I understand loss. Having someone you love die or leave is really hard." The hardest thing Phoebe had ever had to deal with.

"I can tell my dad is sad, too, but he never talks about it." She nibbled on her bottom lip. "He tried yesterday when we talked in Molly's store. But...I can tell he isn't comfortable opening up or showing me how he's really feeling."

Not surprising at all, from what Phoebe knew of Carson; he clearly had an iron fist around his emotions at all times. "I'm guessing he wants to be strong for you," she said, putting a positive spin on Carson's motivations.

"Yeah." Heidi reached down and ran her fingers through the sand. "But sometimes it seems like he's trying so hard to be strong or whatever he's...forgotten CJ and Mom. Or that he isn't sad at all that they're gone." The last few words ended on a woeful half sob, half sigh.

Phoebe let Heidi's words sink in, and after a few seconds, she saw the direction this conversation was going. Carson was clamming up because he was hurting—perfectly understandable, Phoebe had done the same thing—and Heidi was suffering because her dad was having a hard time opening up. All of that added up to one unhealthy roundabout that neither of them knew how to escape.

And it sure opened Phoebe's eyes to the pitfalls of holding grief in. Maybe she'd learn something here, too.

Because she could relate, the unintentional disconnect between father and daughter almost broke her heart. She was sure Carson didn't recognize the ramifications of how he was dealing with their losses; he was a good dad and would probably be horrified to realize that he was hurting Heidi by staying in such rigid control of his feelings.

Not his objective, she was sure. He always seemed to have Heidi's best interests at heart.

So how to say all this to Heidi, in a way that would help and guide without criticizing Carson? Tricky conversation, for sure; Phoebe would have to tread lightly and use some verbal diplomacy.

With that goal in mind, a vague conversational strategy materialized in her brain. "Sweetie…your dad's a cop, right?"

Heidi nodded.

"Well, cops are trained to control things to protect people."

"Like bad guys and stuff?"

"Exactly." Phoebe put her arms on her knees, leaned forward and picked up a small piece of driftwood. "So guys like your dad, who have to have a lot of control to do their jobs well, sometimes have a tough time when they can't make every little thing right, you know?"

Heidi nibbled on her bottom lip. "I guess I never thought of that."

"So, it would follow that having something happen like losing his son would be really hard for him to deal with." Phoebe fiddled with the driftwood and let that thought sink in.

"That makes sense," Heidi replied. "Especially since CJ was killed by a bad guy."

Shock reverberated through Phoebe, and she struggled not to cry out.

Oh, Lord. I didn't see that one coming. Help me deal.

When the sickening shock dissipated and her brain started working again, one thought charged forward. Obviously, Heidi erroneously thought Carson and Phoebe had covered how CJ had died when, in actuality, they hadn't.

And now…one of the reasons for his reluctance to be her discussion partner became clearer. She didn't know the details of CJ's death, but whatever the case, she couldn't imagine how hard it would be for anyone, much less a lawman like Carson, to talk about and face something as awful as a criminal killing his son.

And on top of that, Carson had lost a wife, and Heidi a mom. Had to be rough. Really rough, dealing with two such terrible blows.

With new understanding she looked at Heidi, sending off empathetic waves she hoped Heidi would hang on to. "Exactly. Losing CJ and your mom must be sensitive subjects, don't you think?"

Heidi shifted on the rock. "Yeah, I guess you're right. I just wish he would talk to me more, you know?" She sniffed. "I miss my brother and my mom."

Phoebe's throat burned. "Have you told him this?" she managed.

"Yeah, and we agreed to tell each other stuff more. But I still feel like he's keeping things in. I think he should be mad at my mom for leaving, but he never says he is, and that's weird."

Undoubtedly, Carson was trying to shield Heidi from whatever dynamic had torn their family apart. Understandable, even though she thought maybe he was cocooning Heidi a bit too much with his good intentions.

Something else occurred to Phoebe. "Are you mad at your mom, too?" she asked gently.

"Yeah, I am," Heidi said solemnly. "Seems like she's only thinking about herself rather than me or Dad."

Hoo, boy, there were some pretty big emotions roiling around here. And while Phoebe sympathized, she wondered about picking at the family's wounds. Who was she to stir all of this up? Truth was, she could barely handle her own grief.

Even so, she wanted to comfort Heidi, so she would. Without trying to play psychologist.

"Have you told your dad all of this stuff?" she asked.

"Some of it, but not all. I don't want to make him sadder."

"Don't you think he'd be even more sad if he knew he could have helped you with your sadness and anger, but you didn't tell him?"

"Maybe." Heidi scraped her sun-streaked blond hair

back behind her ear, then turned to Phoebe. "Do you think you could talk to him about this for me?"

"Oh, I don't know," Phoebe said, resisting the urge to refuse outright. *I need You here again, God, to help me do the right thing. What's best for Heidi and Carson. And, yes, for me, too.*

"Please?" Heidi said beseechingly. "I really need some help with this."

Oh, boy. She was between a rock and a hard place, for certain. Phoebe made another attempt to dissuade Heidi, trying to find a balance between being helpful and what Carson might view as meddling. "Your dad might not appreciate me sticking my nose in your business. He's a private guy." As in *very*. Especially when it came to his family. And his feelings.

"But he likes you," Heidi said. "And I think he trusts you, too."

Phoebe's heart rate picked up.

Heidi went on. "I really don't think he'd mind." Heidi turned hopeful eyes up to Phoebe. "Besides, you guys are discussion partners. Aren't you supposed to be helping each other with this kind of stuff?"

Phoebe smiled weakly. Excellent point. One that was hard to refute. "Yes. I guess so."

"Good. Then you can talk to him about this, no problem, right?"

Phoebe sank back, feeling spineless when she realized that putting herself in the middle of Carson and Heidi's business might be a big problem, both for herself and Carson. *Might* being the key word.

A big black hole of uncertainty loomed in front of her, and there wasn't much she disliked or dreaded more. But Heidi needed her help, and Phoebe would have to be heartless not to give the troubled girl what she needed.

Time to grow a spine and face her fear of the unknown. For Heidi.

"Right, no problem," she said, hoping she didn't sound as reluctant as she felt. No sense in freaking Heidi out.

"Maybe you could come over for dinner tomorrow and you guys could talk while I do my homework," Heidi said. "We have pizza every Sunday night."

Phoebe swallowed. "Why don't you run it by your dad, and we'll see, okay?" Maybe Carson would nix the whole idea. Then again, maybe not. Either way, she'd deal.

"Okay, I'll talk to him as soon as he gets home from work." Heidi rose and brushed the sand off her jeans, her mouth pressed into what looked like the first genuine smile Phoebe had ever seen her give. "But I'm sure he'll say yes."

Phoebe got up, too, clutching the piece of driftwood in her hand with a death grip. "Just let me know, then."

"I will."

"Great," Phoebe replied. What was the worst that could happen by accepting Heidi's tentative invitation? Phoebe immediately regretted the loaded question. Because she had a feeling she wouldn't like the answer.

* * *

"She's here!" Heidi excitedly called from the front room, where she'd been camped out for the last half hour, waiting for Phoebe to arrive.

"Go ahead and answer the door." Carson set the plates out on the counter, feeling a not entirely unexpected, yet alarming jolt of adrenaline shoot through him at the thought of Phoebe being here.

Chagrined, he rubbed his jaw, hoping he hadn't made a mistake by agreeing when Heidi had asked yesterday to have Phoebe over for pizza. He couldn't help but wonder, as usual, how smart it was to get any more enmeshed in Phoebe's life than he already was. Discussion partners was one thing; getting her further involved with family affairs was another matter entirely.

But he hadn't had the heart to say no to Heidi, especially since she'd come home yesterday from working at the parlor chattering happily about how Phoebe had let her work the cash register, and how she'd been able to interact with all of the customers. Funny how Heidi had gone from grumbling about working with Phoebe to loving it.

His daughter seemed to be blossoming into a happy kid before his eyes. Nothing pleased him more.

As he gathered the silverware, he admitted he had to hand it to Phoebe. Whatever she was doing during her time spent with Heidi was having a positive influence on his daughter, and if he could foster more good feelings in Heidi by hosting a pizza party with Phoebe, bring the pizza on. Boatloads of it if necessary.

He might be clueless about a lot of things, but even a slow study like himself saw the benefits of having a kind, giving woman like Phoebe involved in Heidi's life.

Benefits for Heidi, sure thing. And what about for him? Worry rose at that reservation, but he batted it down, determined to stay on the peaceful path of least resistance, which, at the moment, was the best he could do given the drama Heidi had brought on lately.

He put the silverware on the table, resisting the strong urge to head out and greet Phoebe. Heidi could handle it.

He heard the front door open, and then Phoebe's voice drifted to him, all soft and melodic. He stood for a moment, willing his heart rate to calm down. What was it about her that intrigued him so? Apart from the fact that she was a truly good person, which even on its own would probably qualify in his mind.

Whatever the case, his goal tonight was to have a casual dinner with Phoebe and Heidi along with a little light conversation and camaraderie, strictly to make Heidi happy. Mission noted.

Heidi came into the kitchen. Phoebe followed and gave him a little wave, lighting up the room with her smile and sparkling, bright blue eyes.

He kept his wits enough to notice she had on slender black jeans, flat little black shoes and a pale pink T-shirt and short black sweater that hugged her curves just right. Her hair was pulled up into a ponytail with a few curly tendrils escaping around her face, and the style emphasized her high cheekbones and delicately curved jawline.

He resisted the urge to stare; she always looked great, but seeing her in the here and now, not dressed in practical ice cream parlor work clothes, gave new meaning in his mind to the word *pretty*.

Actually, the word was *gorgeous*.

Reminding himself of his that-would-be-that plan for the evening, he went into casual host mode. "Hey, there. Glad you could come." And, suddenly, he *was* glad. Go figure.

"Hey to you, too," she said, handing him a large, covered square dish.

"What's this?"

"I brought some of my mom's famous caramel brownies."

"What? No ice cream?" he said with a wink.

Phoebe waved a hand in the air. "Nah. I don't bring my work home."

"Fair enough." He looked at a beaming Heidi. "We love brownies, don't we, sweetie?"

"Uh-huh. But we only ever make the kind that come from a box," Heidi said, making a face.

"True," he replied, his attention back on Phoebe. "I have to admit, I'm not much of a cook. I rely on Mrs. P. for cuisine."

"Well, I'm sure she does a wonderful job," Phoebe

said. "If you remind me, I'll write down the recipe so she can make them."

"Thanks, that'd be great." He set the brownies on the counter. "Mrs. P. loves trying new recipes."

Phoebe craned her head to look at the oven. "The pizza smells fantastic." She grinned in a teasing sort of way. "Homemade?"

"Take and bake," Carson replied, trying not to let her cute smile disarm him too much. "It's Heidi's favorite, and the limit of my pizza cooking skills."

Phoebe gave him a thumbs up. "Sounds perfect," she said. "I love anything I don't have to make."

"I feel exactly the same way," he replied.

The buzzer went off, and Carson took the Hawaiian pizza from the oven and set it on a hot pad on the table. Heidi took care of beverages while he grabbed the salad from the fridge. Within minutes he was seated at the round kitchen table flanked by Heidi on his left and Phoebe on his right.

A cozy family picture indeed. He started to sweat.

He served the pizza while everyone helped themselves to salad. To his surprise, the pizza had barely hit Heidi's plate before she dug in with gusto usually reserved for competitive eaters.

"Hungry?" he asked her before he took a bite of his pizza, one brow hoisted high.

Her mouth full, Heidi nodded and said something that sounded vaguely like "starving," but he couldn't be sure.

"Well, even if you haven't eaten in a year, you still

have to have good manners," he informed her in his helpful-yet-corrective parent voice. "We have a guest."

In midchew, Heidi looked to Phoebe eating her slice of pizza in a very civilized way, no wolfing whatsoever involved. Obviously, Heidi wanted Phoebe to confirm that she agreed with him.

Carson turned and looked at Phoebe, too, interested to see how she'd react to being put on the spot.

Her eyes wide, Phoebe finished chewing, then put her pizza down, picked up her napkin from her lap and daintily wiped her mouth. "Um...what your dad said."

And she passed the on-the-spot test with flying colors.

Heidi put her slice of pizza down and finished chewing. "Okay," she said. "I get the message."

"Thank you," he said, tilting his head to the side. "So," he went on to Phoebe. "Who's minding the store?"

She took a sip of water. "Tanya and her daughter, who occasionally helps out when we need it. It'll be busy, but Tanya's been with me for quite a while, so I'm sure they'll be fine."

"Is she your only employee?"

"Yes. We handle the workload pretty well between the two of us." Phoebe looked at Heidi. "By the way, speaking of Tanya, I have to pass on a compliment to you."

Heidi blinked over her glass of orange juice, then put it down. "You do?"

Nodding, Phoebe said, "Yup. Tanya told me how well she thought you did yesterday at the cash register." She put her napkin back on her lap. "She said you have great customer-service skills, and that you were an expert at counting out change."

Fatherly pride spread through Carson.

A slow smile made its way across Heidi's face. "She said that?"

Phoebe held up her hands. "I'm not making it up."

"Wow," Heidi said. "Cool."

"It's very cool," Carson said, impressed by how Phoebe had made a point of passing along some kudos to Heidi; he had a feeling Phoebe's praise was just the thing to lift Heidi's spirits.

He reached out and squeezed Heidi's hand. "I'm proud of you, honey."

"You should be," Phoebe added. "Working with the public isn't always easy."

Heidi nodded as she popped a stray piece of pineapple into her mouth. "Remember that old man who told me I gave him the wrong change when I didn't?"

"What I remember was how you patiently recounted it for him while remaining polite," Phoebe remarked. "You handled the situation just right."

"Thanks." Heidi beamed.

Her smile was the best thing Carson had seen in a long time.

He sat back in his chair for a moment while Phoebe and Heidi talked about some of the other customers they'd helped yesterday, including a brief discussion about a boy who'd come in who Heidi knew from school.

As they chattered away, he had to admit he liked the vibe happening here. He and Heidi had had a lot of silent dinners lately, just the two of them sitting across the table from each other, with little, it seemed, to say. Or maybe they'd had lots to say, and no idea how to say it. Either way, actually interacting during a meal was much better.

Amazingly, he had Phoebe to thank for that at this meal. She and Heidi really clicked, and in his mind, that connection was priceless, no matter how much it had scared him at first.

Well, still *did* scare him, actually. He'd have to do his best to manage those feelings in the future.

He helped himself to a second slice of pizza, his appetite good for the first time in a long while, and was content to just listen to Phoebe and Heidi talk about girly stuff.

As the conversation went on, Carson's chest tightened. Susan called only occasionally to talk to Heidi, and those conversations were understandably strained and, therefore, superficial. It was as if Susan's grief had obliterated any mothering instincts she'd ever had.

He didn't understand that reaction, but that didn't stop him from seeing how Susan's inability to connect with Heidi affected his daughter; Heidi obviously profoundly missed having another female to interact with. It helped having Lily, and now Phoebe, around.

It didn't take a genius to realize that not having a mother figure in Heidi's life had created a huge void that would be hard, if not impossible, for him to fill. And with Heidi growing up before his eyes—as had been highlighted by the boy conversation of a few minutes ago—well, having no mom around would only get harder for both him and Heidi.

He veered away from that troubling thought, not sure how to rectify that situation without going to a place he wasn't ready to face.

But somehow he knew he'd have to gut up and deal with the situation head-on eventually. Time would march on.

What about his life?

Bothered by the course of his thoughts, he resolutely cleared his mind of anything except simply enjoying the evening spent with Phoebe and Heidi.

Relaxing a bit, he munched on his pizza and salad as the subject of nail polish was covered in-depth by the two ladies gracing the table on either side of him.

To his surprise, a couple of minutes later, Heidi rose, her plate in hand. "May I be excused?"

He dropped his chin, then looked at her plate. One lone crust—which he usually finished off—sat there. "Is that all you're going to eat?" True, she'd eaten fast. But only one slice from a girl who regularly put away three? Hmm.

She shrugged. "I'm saving room for brownies."

"Don't you want to stick around with our guest?" he asked, gesturing with a tilt of his head to Phoebe.

"I have *homework,* remember?" Heidi said.

"I thought you finished it all this afternoon," he said.

Heidi pushed her chair in. "Um…I did. I thought. But then I remembered some reading I…um, have to do for my book report." She paused, chewing on her cheek, and then hastily added, "That's due at the end of the week."

He frowned. Something was fishy. Heidi was normally the kid leaving all of her homework until the very last minute; procrastination was her middle name. Maybe she was turning over a new leaf? One could only hope.

He'd go with that optimistic attitude because he had no other ideas. "Can't you do it after Phoebe leaves?" he asked. "It seems a bit rude to take off right now."

Heidi gave him a blank look, as if she hadn't anticipated his reaction—or maybe she had and was acting puzzled—he couldn't tell which. Before he could figure out what she was up to, she turned and pointedly looked at Phoebe. Kind of like…Phoebe was going to rescue her from some kind of conversational hazard…

What was *that* little nonverbal communication all about? Were they in cahoots about…what? And if so, why?

He tried to gather his muddled thoughts so he could voice his questions, but Phoebe cleared her throat first, beating him to the punch. "Er…I don't mind," she said with a wave of her hand. "Homework always comes first, right?"

How could he refute that statement when she was technically correct? "Right, right." He looked at Heidi. "Go ahead, honey, and come back in a little while for dessert."

"Okay," Heidi said brightly as she scampered off. "See ya later."

Carson watched her go, tapping his finger on the table, the wheels whirring around in his head. In his humble opinion, she looked much too happy to be leaving her new best friend Phoebe quite so eagerly. And right in the middle of a discussion about nail polish, no less. Weird.

Slowly, he moved his gaze to Phoebe, hoping for a clue as to what was going on. No surprise, really, that she was pointedly studying the half-eaten piece of pizza on her plate as if it were encrusted with rare jewels.

Not so suddenly, he had the unmistakable feeling that being left alone with Phoebe so that Miss Suddenly Not a Procrastinator could do some phantom homework had a very distinct purpose.

A niggling of dread skittered through him. He sensed a personal discussion coming on. That, or Heidi wanted him and Phoebe to have some romantic alone time and had somehow conned—or tricked—Phoebe into agreeing. Whatever the case, Heidi's apparent scheming wasn't a good sign.

"Care to tell me what's up?" he asked Phoebe.

She gave him an awkward smile. "I'm not sure you want to know."

The niggling turned into a full-fledged jab that had his brows slamming together and his stomach dropping to his toes. He wasn't sure he wanted to know what was going on, either.

But what choice did his pragmatic self have but to hear Phoebe out?

Chapter Eleven

"If looks could speak, I'd say you're not very happy to be having this conversation," Phoebe said, going for honesty. What was the use in burying her head at this point? She needed to breathe eventually.

He shook his head. "You'd be right."

"I don't blame you, really." She took a sip of water, letting her comment sink in for a second. "Heidi obviously has an agenda that you're not aware of, and that has to be pretty confusing."

"To say the least," he commented dryly. "Care to fill me in?"

There was no way around bringing him into the loop. She fiddled with her fork. "Heidi rushed through her dinner on purpose."

"No kidding. She ate so fast I'm surprised she didn't choke and keel over from lack of oxygen," he said, motioning to his throat.

Phoebe smiled at his attempt at levity. "Yes, well,

I'm pretty sure she was hurrying so you and I would be alone."

"Because?" he asked levelly. Too levelly, as if he were trying to keep rigid control, which, knowing him, he was.

Here went nothing. Or everything? Yikes. "Because she and I talked yesterday, and she asked me to talk to you about…some things."

He sat back and drew his ankle up to rest on the opposite knee, striking a casual pose. Or…a *trying to be* casual pose? "Why don't you just cut to the chase," he said. "I can handle it."

Taking him at his word, she nodded and continued on. "All right. Heidi and I talked about how I understood how sad she felt about her brother's death because I felt the same way about my fiancé's death."

Carson visibly stilled. "Go on."

"And…the conversation came around to how she didn't think you understood how sad and angry she is."

His face knotted. "Why would she think that?" he asked, his voice laced with incredulity.

"Because you never talk about those emotions?"

He stared at her, saying nothing, which said much more than any words possibly could; clearly, she'd hit him with something he didn't want to acknowledge.

She forced herself to go on, wanting to get everything out on the table quickly, kind of like the need to rip a bandage off fast to minimize the trauma. "And because when you never talk about being sad or mad, it makes her feel as if you aren't sad or mad at all."

After a long pause, he cleared his throat and said, "I lost my son." He blinked quickly, then looked down for a second. When he looked back up, his eyes glittered. "How could I not be sad?"

His reaction, while completely appropriate and expected, socked her in the gut. Struggling to breathe, she reached out and touched his hand briefly, wanting to show her support.

"Carson, I'm not saying you're not sad. I know you are, truly I do, and I think deep down Heidi knows, too. What I'm saying is that it *appears* on the surface you aren't sad because you're doing a lot to cover it up."

He jerked in his chin and opened his mouth, then quickly clamped it shut.

She went on, wanting everything out on the table. "Well, while we're on tricky subjects, I should also tell you that Heidi has a lot of anger toward her mom."

His jaw slack, Carson blinked.

"And she feels like her mom's only thinking about herself rather than you and Heidi."

He swiped a hand over his face. "Whoa."

"Yeah, sorry for laying so much on you at once. But this is how your daughter is feeling, so I'm guessing she's pretty overwhelmed about all of her emotions, too."

He slumped back in his chair. "I feel terrible she hasn't felt like she could talk to me about this stuff."

"She told me she doesn't want to make you sadder."

"I'm not quite sure what to say to that."

"Really?"

"You're full of tough questions today, aren't you?" he said, his jaw noticeably tight.

Was his query a delay tactic, to keep from having to open up? Or was he suspicious of her intentions? Or both?

She couldn't do much about the former; Carson was Carson, and she was sure admitting to what she'd called him on wouldn't be easy for him. But the latter? She could definitely do something about that, and it was time to set the record straight so he'd be sure of the motives behind the probing questions she was asking him.

She gave him her most sincere look. "I'm not asking to pry. I'm asking because I care about Heidi, and I promised her I'd talk to you about this. I'm not one to break a promise or make one I can't keep."

His jaw softened, and he looked right at her with those stunning coffee-colored eyes of his.

Her tummy tumbled, and she felt as if she'd suddenly been plunked on a very fast rollercoaster.

"I know," he said. "And I appreciate the interest you've taken in my daughter." He shook his head. "It's just it's never been easy for me to talk about my feelings."

"I understand," she said, hoping truthful commiseration would put him at ease a bit. "But I'm sure once you think about how your reluctance to talk affects Heidi, you'll do the right thing."

"You have an awful lot of faith in me," he replied, sounding awed.

His statement sank in, and the rollercoaster she was stuck on went back up, flinging her into the stratosphere of *oh, my goodness, he's right!* She *did* have a lot of faith in him; he was a good man, a good father and a good person all rolled into one very appealing package. But she'd do her best not to think about that right now, even though she had a feeling she wouldn't be able to ignore the true Carson forever.

"Yes, I do," she said honestly. "Does that surprise you?"

"It does, because I don't deserve your faith," he said in a soft voice that ran its fingers over her heartstrings.

Phoebe sucked in a mental breath, holding back the word *why.* Did she really want to know what secrets lurked inside of Carson?

Yes. Yes, she did. It was easier to avoid conflict; she'd played the avoidance card in the past to keep herself on the familiar, safe path. But somehow she knew Carson and Heidi deserved better from her, and she deserved better, too.

For the first time since Justin had died, she wanted the whole, gut-wrenching truth, no matter how high the rollercoaster flung her. Or how low.

But a bigger question nagged at her. Why the sudden turnaround? Why was she willing to put her emotions on the line with Carson and Heidi? To risk upsetting the carefully crafted status quo of her life? To risk falling for someone whose job put them in danger, just as Justin's had?

The answer was simply too life changing to consider.

Even so, she couldn't turn back now. And she wasn't sure she wanted to.

As silence stretched out, Carson watched the play of emotions on Phoebe's face. Subtle surprise. Introspection. Resolve? Or acceptance?

"I'm going to clear the table." He got to his feet, suddenly restless, gut-punched.

How could he have messed things up with Heidi so badly?

He started gathering the dishes, bracing himself for the difficult conversation to come. Good or bad, he'd opened the door to a confession with his declaration about not deserving Phoebe's faith, and, consequently, would have to find a way to make himself step through.

As he set the dishes on the counter, he realized that something about Phoebe's gentle way of approaching their discussions seemed to draw him out in a manner no one else ever had. He wasn't sure what to make of that realization, but something inside of him told him he could trust her with anything.

Even what had happened with CJ. And his irrevocable part in that tragic event. Not to mention why Susan had left him.

Wow. Pretty big stuff for a private guy like himself. Huge, actually. What was it about this woman that made him want to share his secret shame with her? Aside from the fact that she was warm, witty, kind and caring, and a host of other fascinating things he probably had yet to discover?

He turned the faucet on to rinse the plates, his brain churning from his disquieting thoughts, but then his introspection was brought to a quick halt by a warm touch on his arm that sent tingles throughout him.

He regarded Phoebe, who was looking at him with those bright yet soft blue eyes of hers. "Would you care to elaborate on that statement now?" she asked, her tone as gentle as a breeze, yet strong, too. Amazing how she did that.

"I guess I have to, don't I?"

"No," she replied, shaking her head. "You don't."

He pulled in his chin at her unexpected words and gave her an inquiring look.

"But I think you should." She sucked in a large breath. "I think you're holding something big in."

She was so right. He put his hands on the counter and gazed out the window above the sink, not seeing much, wondering if he was truly ready to reveal the guilt he carried inside of him. "Why do you say that?" he asked, stalling.

Phoebe was silent for a moment. "Heidi told me that a bad guy killed CJ."

His heart tightened so painfully in his chest he

almost let out a gasp. "She shouldn't have said anything," he said through stiff lips.

"Please don't be mad at her," Phoebe said. "She really needed someone to talk to about this, and I'm glad she was comfortable enough for me to be that someone."

He nodded, letting his anger go in the face of her concern for Heidi. "I'm glad, too."

After a beat of silence, Phoebe said, "Carson, what happened to CJ?"

Pressing his lips together and turning off the faucet, he said, "Let's go sit down in the family room."

Phoebe followed him to the couch situated adjacent to the fireplace and settled in beside him, close, but not touching. To his surprise, she held out her hand for him to hold.

After a hesitation, he took it, feeling as if she were handing him a lifeline. Support. Something extraordinary that had been missing from his life for a long time.

"So. Tell me what happened," she said, squeezing his hand.

He fought against the burn in his throat. "CJ was five, and he loved to go to a certain park in Seattle that had a corkscrew slide. So I took him there on my day off to play." CJ had been so happy, so carefree that day.

"We had a great time, and it was a rare really warm summer day, so we walked to a convenience store a couple of blocks away to get slushies." He looked off into space, blinking. "He loved the ones that made his tongue turn blue."

"I loved that flavor, too, when I was growing up," Phoebe said.

He geared himself up to finish his story. "We were in the back filling our cups, and suddenly there was a commotion up front by the register." Carson closed his eyes as horrific memories assaulted him. Sucking in a shaking breath, he continued. "I turned and observed a guy wearing a black hat pointing a gun at the cashier."

Phoebe clutched his hand and remained silent.

"My training kicked in, and as a cop, I couldn't stand by and let a robbery happen right under my nose without trying to do something. So I led CJ into the back room by the slushy machine and told him to stay where he was."

He heard Phoebe sniff, but he couldn't look at her, couldn't see the condemnation in her eyes if he had any hope of getting the rest of his tale out.

"He hesitated and looked up at me, so scared, and I told him to pay attention to me and to be quiet." He let out a harsh breath. "I should have listened to what he was trying to tell me—that he was frightened and needed me to stay with him. But I thought he was safe in the back room, away from the danger—right?—and I made a snap decision I don't think I can ever forgive myself for."

Phoebe remained silent as she pulled his hand into her lap and gripped it even tighter, with both hands now.

He clenched back, drawing strength from her touch. "I wasn't carrying, so my plan was to somehow disarm the perp by tackling him from behind. So I crept out of the back room and around the aisle and came up on him from the rear of the store."

What happened next was burned into his brain like some ghastly tableau that he would never forget for as long as he lived. "Just as I got close enough to attack, I heard a noise to my left. I looked at the perp, and saw his head turn toward the noise." Carson looked down, tears burning his eyes. "And then he swung his gun left and fired three shots—*bam, bam, bam*—and I launched myself at him, tackling him just as he got the last shot off."

Tears streamed down his cheeks, and he made no effort to wipe them away. "But I was too late."

"Oh, Lord, no," he heard Phoebe utter.

He forced himself to say, "Yes. CJ had come out of the back room, and was looking for me." A sob escaped from his lips. "The perp shot him, and my boy died before he hit the ground, and I might as well have been the one who pulled the trigger."

Phoebe's hand tightened spasmodically on his, gripping him so hard he was sure she was cutting off his circulation. Dead silence filled the room as he hung his head and let the tears come. "I haven't cried since that day," he whispered hoarsely, his chest squeezing, making talking difficult. "Not one single tear."

"Why is that, do you think?" Phoebe asked in a thick voice.

"I don't deserve the release." Hard truth, for sure. But he believed that reality with every cell in his body. "CJ will never shed another tear, or laugh or sigh in wonder. Why should I be able to find comfort in doing the same?"

"Oh, Carson," Phoebe said, pulling on his hand.

He gave in to the pressure and turned and leaned toward her. Her arms went around him and pulled him close. All that was Phoebe surrounded him, comforted him and eased just a bit of his pain.

Something inside of him shifted, and he felt his walls tremble. Some of the tightness in his chest eased, releasing its stranglehold. He hugged her tight and let more tears flow as her hands rubbed his back in a soothing motion.

Was it possible he'd found something in this wonderful woman he hadn't even known he'd been looking for?

She hitched in a breath, then pulled away slightly and cupped his chin in her hand, forcing him to look at her. She gently wiped the wetness from his face. Fat tears ran down her cheeks, as well. It seemed only natural to do the same for her, so he tenderly ran his fingers over her cheeks, sweeping away the remnants of her tears.

"You are not responsible for CJ's death," she said, looking deep into his eyes.

Unable to face her, accept what she was saying, he turned away. "I shouldn't have left him."

Forcing him to look at her again, she said, "You thought he was safe."

"I shouldn't have left him," he repeated in a strangled voice. "I should have known not to leave him by himself, and I'll never forgive myself for that."

After a poignant pause, she touched his cheek again. "God forgives you."

He froze, taken aback by her statement; his religious education was nonexistent, and his thought process didn't usually include God in the equation. "How do you know?" he asked, curious. He was optimistic, maybe, about something that had never brought him any measure of hope.

"'In him we have redemption through his blood, the forgiveness of sins, in accordance with the riches of God's grace.'"

"Somehow I don't think those are your words."

"You're right." She dropped her hand to his shoulder and squeezed. "It's a quote from the Bible."

"That's what I figured, but I'm not familiar with biblical quotes."

"Well, maybe you should get familiar with the wisdom in the Bible."

"Why?" he asked, intrigued.

"It can be very comforting in difficult times to be

assured that God is on your side, and that you can always rely on Him for comfort."

Something occurred to him. "Yet it doesn't seem like you're really taking your own advice."

"What?" she asked, her forehead creasing.

"Relying on God for comfort," he said, hoping he wasn't overstepping his bounds by calling her on ignoring her own counsel. But somehow, after all they'd talked about, pointing out the flaws in her reasoning seemed fitting.

She yanked in her chin, then stood abruptly. "What do you mean?"

"Well, obviously you go to church."

Nodding with one brow raised, she said, "Y-yes. Until recently, at least."

"And obviously you know the Bible's teachings, because you just quoted directly from it."

"Yes," she said, looking at him sideways, doubt etched across her features.

"So are you getting any comfort from Him, or the Bible?"

She flushed. "This conversation is about you, not me."

"Don't change the subject."

She pursed her lips, getting ready, he was sure, to deny his words.

He held up a hand and stood, then walked over to face her. "Don't even try denying what you're doing. I'm an expert on the benefits of subject changing, so I know when someone is doing it."

She dropped her head again. "Busted."

He had to smile. "So I take it you agree that this conversation is about both of us?"

Her mouth trembling, she stared at him, her still-damp eyes wide. Finally she said, "I don't know if I can talk about this."

"Your words are mine," he said, moving closer. He took her hand, felt it tremble. "And that breaks my heart."

Tears crested in her eyes and trickled down her cheeks. "This is too hard."

"I know," he said, nodding, his own eyes burning again. "But someone once told me that talking about painful things can help."

"My own words, coming back to haunt me," she said, rolling her eyes. "Figures."

"Only because they were smart words." He reached up and put one hand on each of her shoulders. "Talk to me."

She looked at the floor, then took a deep breath as if she were steeling herself to say something momentous. "I'm angry with God for taking Justin away," she whispered so softly he could barely hear her.

"Go on," he managed.

"And…there's a chasm between me and Him, and I don't know how to fix it."

Something the police department psychiatrist had told Carson clicked into place. "Don't take this the wrong way, but is it possible you don't want to fix it?"

She frowned, then pulled away and backed up a few steps, crossing her arms over her middle. "Meaning?"

He tried to remember what the shrink had told him. "Well, sometimes we shy away from doing things, and the pulling back is so subconscious we don't even know we're doing it."

He had a feeling this applied to him, too, and that by talking about it, he'd have some truths of his own to face. All in good time. Maybe. Pointing it out to someone else and admitting it applied to him were two very different things.

"Okay," she said, nodding warily. "So how does that apply to me?"

He hoped he could say this right; he was treading in new territory right now, and he'd never been good at expressing himself verbally. "Your anger at God is serving a purpose right now—to protect you from acknowledging your pain. So it stands to reason that if you're not angry at Him anymore, you have to face what's hurting you."

"And that is...?" she asked in a paper-thin whisper.

"Your loss."

His last word echoed in the room like a silent yet deadly blast. Phoebe stood, frozen. "I've...never thought about it that way."

"Neither have I, even though someone I saw after CJ died pointed the same thing out to me a while ago." Although he'd been so broken up about CJ's death, he hadn't heard most of it. Or, hadn't wanted to.

"But you didn't listen?" she asked.

He shook his head and moved toward Phoebe until he stood right in front of her. "I wasn't ready to." Was he ready now? And if so, why?

Because of Phoebe? Oh, man. What was he doing, letting her be a catalyst for changes that scared him more than facing down a gang of armed punks on the street?

"Maybe I haven't been ready yet, either," she said, drawing his thoughts away from the dangerous road up ahead he couldn't seem to veer from. "Admitting I've been using my anger to work against my relationship with God is a hard thing to accept."

"I know." And he did. Too well, he was realizing. Because he would have to accept some hard truths about himself.

She gave him a questioning stare.

"I've been doing the same thing, only my anger is directed at myself, not God." Profound words, for sure. And life changing, he suspected.

He diverted his attention away from his own chaotic questions and looked at Phoebe. She had her brow furrowed, and he could see the cogs turning in her brain.

His heart rate skittered; her putting it all together meant he'd set himself up to be called on his own behavior and had realized it too late.

Or maybe just in time?

"So," she said, raising her chin. "What we can take away from this is that I need to let my anger at God go in order to forgive Him, to repair the chasm between Him and me."

"Yep." But there was more, much more.

She confirmed this realization by saying, "And you need to let your anger at yourself go to forgive yourself."

He swallowed, wondering if it had been wise to even step on this road. Guess he was already on it. "Yes, I believe that about covers it," he managed.

After a significant pause, she reached out and took his hand in hers. Warmth radiated from her touch, warmth that sucked him in, despite his best efforts to fight its draw.

"I'm willing to admit you have a point and that I'll try to work on not using my anger against God in the interest of healing the rift between Him and me."

"Great," he said, pretty sure she wasn't finished. Unfortunately for him. Or…not. And…why couldn't he tell the difference anymore? Talk about confused. "Good for you."

"So if it's so great, let me ask you one more question," she said.

"Shoot," he replied, fearing her response like the bullet his word implied.

She looked directly at him, and for the life of him, he couldn't look away.

"Are you willing to do the same in the interest of forgiving yourself for CJ's death?" she asked, her voice gentle. And her statement? Not so much, though he wasn't holding that against her.

Kudos to her for asking the tough questions.

As he rattled to a bumpy, painful halt at his chaotic

destination, he had to own up to her question, which, while not unexpected, nevertheless homed in on the crux of the matter: Could he forgive himself? And if he did, and that huge step helped him to look deeper, what would he learn about his desire to have Phoebe in his life?

He let out a long breath. Phoebe had said this opening-up stuff wasn't going to be easy.

Too bad she was right.

Chapter Twelve

To Phoebe, Carson's body language—tight jaw, furrowed brow—screamed *uncomfortable*.

So she pulled away to allow him to think; if he were as distracted by her closeness as she was by his, he wasn't going to be able to respond to her pointed query about forgiving himself at all coherently.

Would he even respond at all? She knew how hard it was to ask oneself the tough questions, much less respond to someone else asking. She wouldn't be at all surprised if he told her to butt out and mind her own business.

Well, maybe a tad surprised...

Bothered by the possibility that he might tell her to take a hike, she wandered over and looked out the window to her right, noting the wooden deck flanked by an overgrown backyard. Apparently Carson didn't have much time for yard work. No surprise there; as the sheriff and single parent he probably didn't have time for anything but work and being a dad.

He obviously had a full plate. Even so, he'd taken time to invite her over and talk, to include her in his and Heidi's lives. Somehow that made her insides all warm and mushy. And distinctly conflicted.

What else was new since the handsome sheriff had walked into the parlor to talk about Heidi? Seemed Phoebe would be used to the topsy-turvy emotions father and daughter brought out in her.

Her thoughts were interrupted by Carson's cell phone ringing.

A pause. "Hello?" he said.

Phoebe turned around.

Carson listened for a moment, nodding, and then said, "No problem. I'll be there shortly." He disconnected and shoved his phone back into his pocket. "That was Deputy Miller. I'm needed at the station."

Good timing. For both of them. "Okay. Do you want me to stay with Heidi?"

"Mrs. P. is always willing to come on short notice."

"It seems silly to bother her on a Sunday. Why don't you go, and I'll hang out here with Heidi. I'm sure she'll be down after she finishes her homework."

He gave Phoebe a gentle smile. "You sure?"

"Absolutely." And maybe it would be better if she had some time to process what they'd talked about. Maybe a couple of years would be long enough. Then again, maybe not.

"Okay. Thanks." He headed over and grabbed his

keys from a ceramic bowl on the counter. "I shouldn't be long."

"Take your time," she said, meaning it. She had a lot to think about.

He left, and she was alone with nothing but her thoughts, which were anything but serene. Especially since Carson had told her how CJ had died, which had cracked her heart wide open, like a broken egg oozing through her. Just the thought of what he'd gone through, and the guilt and self-reproach he carried around like a stone on his back, made her chest ache and her eyes water.

She pressed a hand to the bridge of her nose to keep herself from crying. Inevitably, she thought about the fact that they both struggled with forgiveness. Amazing that they shared that bond. But frightening, too, for someone like her who preferred neat and tidy emotions she could manage.

But this…this whirlpool of confusion and shifting emotions and slippery-slope changes made her feel vulnerable. As if her heart had a target etched on it and Carson and Heidi were trading off shooting arrows at her.

Sooner or later, Phoebe feared one of them would hit a bull's-eye that would not only hurt, but would change her forever.

What if she let herself love Carson and Heidi, and she lost them? How would she survive that?

She pressed a hand to her chest, feeling an achy

fullness in her heart that told her that one—or both—of them had already landed a near-perfect shot to her center. And that no matter what happened, her heart would never be the same now that the Winterses were in her life.

Three hours after he'd left, Carson pulled his cruiser back into the driveway, both glad and apprehensive that Phoebe was still here.

What a weird, unsettling way to feel, this odd combination of happiness and nervousness that always seemed to take ahold of him when she was around. How could one woman manage to stir so many conflicting emotions inside of him?

He sat for a moment, allowing himself to go back to the conversation he and Phoebe had had before he'd been called away. He had to say, he admired how she'd turned his suggestion about forgiving God back on him. Coming at him from that angle had helped the concept of forgiving himself make more sense, even though her right-back-atcha had forced him to look things in the eye he'd rather stuff away in a box, never to be viewed.

For the first time since CJ had died, he realized that maybe he needed to change the way he did things, the way he approached his grief. For himself, yes. But especially for Heidi. Anything for her.

Maybe he could even ask God for help? Amazing how that concept, coming from Phoebe, seemed logical, even achievable. Something he could accept and hold on to when the chips were down.

But, then, she was an amazing woman. And he had a feeling he'd just begun to scratch her surface.

He shook his head as he exited his rig, put off-balance by his thoughts of Phoebe. Guess his disorderly emotions had become standard operating procedure since she'd come into their lives.

Letting himself in the door, he noted all of the lights at the front of the house were off and the rooms were quiet and still. Made sense, given the hour. Heidi was surely already asleep. Thank goodness Phoebe had agreed to stay as late as need be when he'd called a few hours ago to tell her he was going to be longer than he'd originally thought.

He stopped in his office and locked up his service weapon, then headed toward the family room and dark kitchen, noting the glow of the TV shining into the hallway. As he entered the room, he looked left, and saw Phoebe stretched out on the couch, asleep. She'd obviously dozed off while watching the tube.

Moving closer, he stared down at her, noting how her curly hair covered one cheek. The light from the TV cast her face in shadows, but there was enough illumination to see the soft curve of her jaw. She had one hand up to cushion her head on the padded end of the microfiber couch, and the other lay relaxed on her hip.

Something warm moved through him as he watched the slight rise and fall of her chest while she slept.

What would it be like to come home to her every night like this? To have her waiting for him?

Intrigued by his train of thought, he resisted the urge to shove the vision into a tight cage; there was no harm in dreaming, was there?

The minute he let down his mental guard he was filled with a yearning he hadn't allowed himself to have in a very long time. A longing for companionship. Support. Love. Someone to come home to after a long day. All things a woman could provide.

A woman like Phoebe.

Shocked at how quickly he'd woven Phoebe into his crazy vision of another life, he reeled himself in, away from the chaos of allowing love into his heart again. What was the use in dreaming of things that had such a price?

But…what was it about this woman that had him envisioning her as a part of this family? Part of his life?

Before he could answer those leading questions, Phoebe stirred, opened her eyes and looked at him. After a blank-look hesitation, she spread her mouth into a slow, sleepy smile that socked him in the chest and made his mouth go dry.

"Hi," she said on a yawn, stretching. "Did you just get home?"

Swallowing, he moved around the couch, feeling weird that she'd caught him watching her sleep. He had to get a grip.

"Yeah. Sorry it took so long. It's not often we book

so many people for drunk and disorderly and MIPs."
A group of underage college kids had come to town
for the weekend and built a bonfire on the beach, then
proceeded to get smashed on beer they'd hauled down
there in a keg. What a mess.

She sat up and smoothed her smushed curls back
with one hand, looking adorable. "MIP?"

"Minor in possession."

"Oh." She rubbed her eyes. "Anyway, it was no
problem. I was watching mindless TV and guess I
dozed off."

"Did everything go okay with Heidi?" he asked, sitting on the end of the couch. Close, but not too close.
Safe. Maybe, though part of him wondered if he'd ever
be safe again.

Phoebe rubbed her eyes, nodding. "Yup. We
watched a show on TV about baby animals, and then
she went to bed at nine like you asked."

"Great. Thanks." He ran a hand through his hair,
then turned to Phoebe, making a snap decision. "I
know it's late, but do you think we could continue the
discussion we were having before I left?" Maybe talking would help answer some of the lingering questions
he had.

She blinked. "Sure." She uncoiled her feet from underneath her. "I think we left off with me asking you
if you could do what you suggested I do and forgive
yourself for CJ's death."

"Trust me, I haven't forgotten what we were talking about," he said ruefully.

"Do you wish you *could* forget?"

"Part of me does." The part that wanted to stay hidden and blissfully clueless. Alone and safe from turmoil.

"But the other part?" she asked.

"The other part realizes that if I truly want to heal, and if I want to help Heidi, I'm going to have to face some hard truths."

She skimmed his arm with her hand. "You've come a long way."

"I have you to thank," he said honestly, trying to ignore the tingles her touch caused. "You've helped me to see that the necessary path isn't always the path of least resistance."

"It's funny you'd say that."

"Why?"

"Because I'm an expert at doing whatever's easiest, even if it may not be best in the long run." She gave him a crooked smile. "I like it when things stay the same."

"Guess we're a lot alike in that way, aren't we?" He cocked a brow. "Always taking the safe route."

"Less chance to get hurt that way," she said.

Exactly. "So what are we going to do about that?"

"Um…open up?"

The prospect had his stomach knotting, but he held out a hand; if she could take the risk, so could he. Plus, she knew how he felt, and that unique bond strengthened his resolve to conquer his fears. For Heidi. "I'm game if you are."

After a slight hesitation, she took his hand, her grasp warm and soft. Comforting. Wonderful. "Game on."

With so much on the line, he only hoped it was a win-win situation for both of them.

For a woman out to maintain her precious status quo, Phoebe was afraid she liked the feel of Carson's hand in hers just a bit too much. What else was new? He always made her want risky things.

She gingerly pulled her hand away, looking for necessary distance, but then missing his touch the second he let go of her. Go figure.

"So. Why don't you go first," she said. Chicken sounds echoed in her head. One baby step at a time for her.

"If I remember correctly, you asked me whether I could forgive myself for CJ's death."

"Actually, what I asked was whether you could work on getting rid of your anger toward yourself in the *interest* of self-forgiveness."

He rubbed his shadowed jaw. "Guess I have to force myself to look at stuff I'd rather ignore."

"Such as?"

A shadow crept into his eyes. "How mad I am at myself for leaving CJ." A pause. "Livid, really, and I hate that. I can never relax, never feel…peaceful."

"So, you're saying you want peace."

He looked away. "More than anything, but I'm afraid I'll never have it, like I'm trapped in this circle of…negativity, anger, grief and chaos, and I don't know how to get out."

His circle comment struck a chord. "So, you want peace, but you're stuck in a circle of anger that leads to denying yourself forgiveness, which leads to chaos, which leads to anger and unhappiness, and the cycle starts over." She took a deep breath. "So the way I see it, you're never going to get the peace you crave until you forgive yourself."

He was silent for a while. Finally he said, "What you've said makes an odd kind of sense. But I truly don't know how to get to a place of self-forgiveness."

"Have you thought any more about asking God for help with that?"

"Actually, I have."

She raised her eyebrows. "Great. I'm impressed." He never quit surprising her.

"One question, though."

"Okay," she said, an odd niggling of dread starting to jab at her.

"How, exactly, can leaning on God help me?" he asked in an even voice.

Seemed like a reasonable question. "I believe that if you have faith in God, you'll be comforted, and that will then, in turn, help you with your grief. And then you'll have peace."

He shifted on the couch until he was fully facing her, his gaze speculative. "So, if having faith in God is such a no-brainer, why don't you have any?"

The veracity of his comment took the wind out of her sails. Sagging back on the couch, she realized this conversation had taken a turn she hadn't expected, but probably should have. Carson was no idiot. And he deserved nothing less than honesty from her.

Trouble was, that meant looking into her heart and accepting that if she wanted to move on—and, surprisingly, now that she'd met Carson, she did—she was going to face some difficult truths.

And she was also going to have to let God back into her life.

Was that particular undertaking going to be much harder than she'd ever imagined?

Carson saw Phoebe's shoulders sag as she crossed her arms over her torso, folding inward. He immediately regretted pushing her about her falling-out with God. She was probably going to tell him to mind his own business in no uncertain terms.

He let the silence play out for a while, and his self-recrimination gradually faded. Phoebe wouldn't want him to pull any punches, given she hadn't pulled any with him. That just wasn't her style. In fact, her straightforwardness was one of the things he liked best about her.

Finally, the strung-out silence got to him. "I guess I've thrown you for a loop, haven't I?" he said, going for semi-neutral ground.

"Not really," she said as she rubbed at what looked to be an imaginary spot on the couch.

"I don't buy that," he said. "You're rarely left speechless, and you rarely fiddle with invisible things on furniture."

With a small smile, she inclined her head to the side and seemingly very deliberately lifted her hand in the air. "True on both counts. The thing is...if I admit you're right, then I'll have to change things, and I'm not sure I'm ready to do that."

"I understand," he replied. "But I don't think there's that much change involved."

She gave him a look brimming with obvious skepticism. "Why not?"

"So you say there's a chasm between you and God, and that you're angry with Him, and you told me that faith helps people through loss by offering comfort, right?"

"Yes."

"So...I contend that faith doesn't just disappear, and that you're in essence ignoring your own beliefs by letting the chasm between you and God affect your relationship with Him."

She looked sideways at him. "I assume there's a point here?"

He turned so he was looking directly at her. "Shouldn't your faith bridge that gap, at least partway?"

She blinked at him, her jaw visibly loosening.

Plunging forward, he added, "At least enough to help you realize how important God is to you, especially now, after you've suffered such a loss?"

She sat staring at him for a long, tense moment, her pretty blue eyes glimmering, her lips quivering.

Regret spilled through him like battery acid; he'd pushed too far. What had he been thinking? Telling others what to do wasn't his usual M.O. In fact, he usually went with the exact opposite and stayed uninvolved.

"I'm sorry," he uttered, shaking his head. "I shouldn't have—"

She placed a finger on his lips, silencing him. "No, don't apologize," she said, her voice raspy.

All he could manage to do was stare unblinkingly at her.

She stared back, her blue eyes wide, hanging on his gaze. And then with a muffled cry, she snaked her arms around his shoulders and hugged him.

Floored, tingling all over, he hesitated for a stunned moment, and then wrapped his arms around her.

"You are so right about everything," she whispered in his ear. "I *have* been using my anger against God instead of relying on my faith and asking Him for help."

Something warm blew up in his chest, taking his breath away. When he was able to draw air in again, he buried his nose in her hair, inhaling the citrus scent of her shampoo, wanting to hold her close and never let her go.

"I only went by what you taught me." He pulled back and cupped her smooth cheek in his hand.

"Looks like we both learned something here today, didn't we?"

She nodded, clinging to him with those liquid blue eyes. He couldn't look away. Couldn't even breathe. Something in his brain misfired, and before he could stop himself, he closed the distance between them.

And then he did what he insisted he wouldn't. He kissed her, full-on, no holding back. She gasped against his lips, and then kissed him back, her mouth soft as silk against his.

A deep feeling of contentment jolted through him, and he realized how much he'd missed being close to a woman in this way. Strangely, it seemed as if an important piece of him that had been gone for a long time fell back into place, completing him in an inexplicable yet staggering way.

After a long, wonderful moment, Phoebe pulled back, staring at him from just inches away. "Wow."

Smiling, he smoothed her hair behind her ear. "Yeah. Wow." As in, completely amazing.

Chewing on her lip, she broke their linked gazes. "Do you think we're making a mistake?" she asked, snuggling down against his side.

He sat back against the couch, pulling her with him. "At the moment, I don't really care."

"Really?" she asked, her voice doused with uncertainty.

Smiling, he squeezed her shoulder. "I know, that sounds weird." To himself, too. What was going on, anyway? Why was he letting himself be pulled into all that was Phoebe? Other than the fact that she was the most wonderful woman he'd ever met?

"Um…yeah." She pushed back so she could give him a hefty look. "Care to explain?"

He thought about it for a few moments, and the answer was suddenly obvious. "I haven't felt this happy in a long time, and I'm not fighting the feeling." After a hesitation, he went on. "Don't you think we both deserve some happiness after what we've been through?"

She stilled, her expression hitting shell-shocked dead center.

He held his breath, and just about the time he was sure he'd gone someplace he shouldn't have, her face softened and she spread her mouth into a captivating smile that hit him even harder than her kiss had.

"You know, you're right," she said, settling back into his arms. "We deserve this."

"I'm so glad you agree," he said, unaccountably relieved she was staying right where she was for the time being. He wasn't ready to let her go.

And right now, with her sitting pressed close, he didn't think he'd ever be willing to allow her to walk out of his life without putting up a fight.

Just as the sun started shining through her bedroom window—which was *early,* given it was May—Phoebe finally gave up on sleep and got out of bed. Quite a feat for a non–morning person such as herself who considered it a major crime to get up at any hour starting with a five. Or six. Or seven.

She'd had a rough night. No matter how many sheep she'd counted, she simply couldn't stop thinking about the handsome sheriff who'd completely turned her world upside down since sauntering into her life.

Bleary-eyed, she put on a fuzzy robe and her favorite pair of slippers. Then she shuffled into the kitchen and made a big pot of coffee and shoved an English muffin into her toaster oven. While her sustenance percolated and browned, she leaned a hip against the counter, unable to ignore what had become unavoidably obvious over the course of the too-short night she'd spent doing I-can't-sleep gymnastics on her mattress.

She was falling for Carson.

And that scared the filling out of her.

With a noisy sigh, she grabbed a glass of orange juice, then got her toasted muffin out and spread peanut butter on it. She made quick work of a banana with a paring knife and put the slices on the muffin, then poured herself a big cup of coffee and took the whole shebang to the small wooden table in the corner of her kitchen.

She sat down, stirred some sugar into her coffee and balefully regarded her peanut butter and banana muffin, curling her lip. Great. Now anxiety had chased her hunger away. Not good at all. She loved to eat—usually.

But this wasn't a usual day following a regular evening; she'd spent a good part of the last evening curled in Carson's arms on his couch, cuddling and talking, and she'd loved every single second of it. He'd been right; he made her happy, and she didn't have it in her to deny that.

Her world was tilting on its side, and was in danger of turning completely upside down.

No wonder she hadn't slept a wink. All she'd thought about while she'd been tossing and turning was what he'd said to her about her faith and God. Sometime before dawn, she'd begun to realize that Carson was right; her faith should have carried her through with God after Justin had died.

Now, despite her lack of rest, she couldn't deny the wisdom in Carson's advice. She had faith, had for a very long time. She needed to trust in God, and that, in turn, should pave the way to being able to bridge the gap that she'd allowed to form between her and Him. She hadn't been able to see the forest for the trees about her problem. Thank goodness Carson had been there to help her realize the error of her ways and show her the forest.

She took a sip of coffee, acknowledging that her realization had come at an excellent time; with her heart in knots over her undeniable feelings for Carson, she was going to need God's guidance more than ever.

Feeling the chasm between her and the Lord lessening, a tentative sense of peace came over her. Casting her eyes up, she folded her hands together on the table. And then she prayed.

God, I'm sorry I lost faith, but I know You will forgive me. I've missed having You in my life, and I need Your guidance. I'm beginning to think letting Carson into my life might be all right, that maybe second chances do exist.

But how do I know for sure?

Chapter Thirteen

After a busy week at the ice cream parlor, Thursday evening rolled around, and Phoebe sat at grief-counseling class, wondering if she'd see Carson here tonight. He'd gone MIA from her life for the past few days since they'd kissed, and for all she knew, grief counseling was no longer on his list.

Funny how she'd become used to having him in her life. She missed him. A lot.

Had he had second thoughts about their relationship? She'd been too much of a wuss to call him and find out.

To her relief—and chagrin—he showed up at the class—late, but *present*—and stood in the back. Trying to act casual, she gave him a wave and a shaky smile, which he returned, and she sat back and listened to the instructor, barely able to sit still. She'd meet with him after class to talk; she'd had her head under the covers long enough. If he had any regrets, she wanted to know about them.

After the instructor went over the seven stages of grief—very enlightening, especially the information about the anger stage—the class broke up, and Phoebe approached him.

"Hey, you. Long time no see," she said, her tummy fluttering. Looked as though he still had the ability to make her giddy.

He flushed. "Yeah, sorry. One of my deputies was out sick, and things have been crazy at the station."

"You sure that's all it is?" she asked, wanting honesty to soothe her own doubts, ridiculous as they might be.

Frowning, he took her arm and gently pulled her out into the hall. "Yes, I'm sure. I've barely seen Heidi, either, though she did tell me she's been helping out at the parlor voluntarily now."

Phoebe nodded. "I'm thrilled Heidi has chosen to continue working at the store."

Searching her face, he asked, "What's going on?"

Guess the honesty thing went both ways. "I just thought maybe you were pulling away after...well, you know, what happened." Her cheeks heated.

He frowned.

"I'd understand that perfectly," she said, forging ahead because if she didn't she'd chicken out and shut down. "We talked about a lot of personal things on your couch, and we, um...kissed. It would stand to reason that you might want to...slow things down." Or stop their relationship completely.

Her heart stuttered. Just the thought of him pulling completely away made her incredibly sad.

"Honestly, the work thing is true. I've been putting in long hours," he said.

She saw the sincerity in his eyes. "I'm being weird, aren't I?" She gave him a wan smile. "I'm not usually quite so doubting."

"No, I *have* been quiet." He touched her arm. "But it was out of necessity. Things have been really busy at work, and I didn't want to call you or stop by when I didn't really have time to talk."

"Okay," she said, believing him completely. She'd been worried for nothing. Yet, her worry alone pointed to some very profound feelings she was going to have to confront.

"But I have time now," he said, gesturing down the hall. "How about we continue our discussion at my house?"

Her spirits rose as she fell into step beside him. "Is Heidi going to be there? I missed seeing her today."

"I'm not sure. She and Lily went shopping earlier, and their timeline was loose."

"Oh, right, now I remember. Heidi told me they were going to the mall in Harbor City."

"Yeah, something about new skinny jeans or something." He shrugged, then held the door open for her. "I'm not in on the details. I just supply the money."

"We girls like to shop," she said, inhaling the fresh ocean breeze, hoping it would clear her head. "You'd better get used to that."

"Oh, trust me, my daughter has already conditioned me for the shopping bug, and I have the credit-card receipts to prove it."

Phoebe laughed. "Just wait until she wants designer jeans and shoes."

"Guess I'll have to put my foot down when that happens."

I hope I'm around to see it, she thought, accepting the truth in her musings. There was no denying the idea. She wanted to be part of Carson and Heidi's lives for a long time to come. She wanted to see Heidi go to the prom, graduate from high school and go off to college. She wanted to see her move into adulthood, get married and have kids of her own someday. She wanted to watch all of those milestones by Carson's side while they built a home and memories together and, someday, became grandparents.

So, what did that mean for herself, in the here and now?

Feeling another heartfelt discussion with God coming on in the near future—my, she liked the sound of having Him to lean on—she decided to table the ramifications of her realization for the time being, choosing instead to focus on the evening at hand and whatever that brought.

They decided to take separate cars so Phoebe could drive directly home from his house later, and Carson followed Phoebe out of town. The mostly sunny day had stayed clear, and as the glowing sun made its way toward the horizon, ribbons of orange and pink streaked the sky to the west. Phoebe looked in her rearview mirror and saw Carson driving his SUV behind her. Steady. Watchful. With her all the way, a presence she couldn't deny.

Something shifted inside of her, and a yearning for that future she'd imagined with Heidi and Carson formed a tight knot of need in her chest that simply could not be denied.

Dare she hope for a future as a real part of the Winters family?

"Surprise!"

As the echoes of all of those gathered for Phoebe's birthday reverberated in the decorated entryway of his house, Carson kept his eyes on Phoebe when they walked through the front door, sure her expression was going to be priceless. Though he never got tired of looking at her pretty face, no matter what emotion she expressed.

Sure enough, her face exploded in utter astonishment, and then morphed quickly into a dazzling smile that made his heart feel as if it were going to float right out of his chest.

She turned to him, her eyes sparkling like sunlit blue topaz. "My birthday isn't for four days!" she said, stabbing the air in front of his nose with a finger. "Nice job getting me here, sneaky!"

"I do my best," he replied with a tilt of his head and a crooked smile. "But most of the credit goes to Heidi."

Phoebe turned as Heidi separated herself from the crowd. "You did all this?" Phoebe gestured around at the crepe paper and balloon-festooned walls.

Heidi nodded, her face lit up by a brilliant, truly happy smile Carson hadn't seen in a long time. "Well, it was my idea, but Lily and Molly helped," she said, gesturing to Phoebe's friends. "And Molly clued me in about your birthday."

Phoebe gave Lily and Molly each a defined, smile-tinged nod of appreciation, then extended her arms and enfolded Heidi in a hug. Heidi hugged back, her face relaxing into a kind of contentment he would never tire of seeing.

With that thought in mind, he stood back and watched them embrace, his throat tightening at the affection so obvious between his daughter and the wonderful woman who'd come into their lives. Clearly, Phoebe had worked her way into the heart of this family.

Powerful stuff, for sure.

Powerful, yet intimidating. Though he'd spoken the truth when he'd told Phoebe the craziness at work had kept him from seeking her out the past few days, in the back of his mind doubts about letting Phoebe into his heart had remained. Especially after their cozy night spent kissing and talking on the couch, which had sent him into a bit of a tailspin, given the emotional intimacy that had pervaded the evening.

Even so, as he'd sat there with Phoebe in his arms

that night, he'd felt so at ease, so centered. So happy. As if he were right where he was supposed to be.

Since that night, however, his inherent desire to avoid messy emotions was at war with his growing need to be with Phoebe, to grab on to the positive feelings she brought out, and never let go.

He was smack-dab in the middle of a push/pull he couldn't seem to break free of.

Work had given him a reason to put his feelings on the back burner for a few days. But now that Deputy Diaz was back from being out with the flu, things at the station were returning to normal, and any legitimate reason Carson might have for keeping Phoebe at arm's length was gone.

It was time to face the feelings staring him down. Whether he liked the idea or not.

The dire course of his thoughts was interrupted by Heidi. "Dad, come with us to go see Phoebe's cake out on the deck!"

"Sure thing, sweetie." He looked at Phoebe, then crooked his arm and presented it to her. "Could the birthday girl please accompany us out back?"

She grinned and laid her hand on his upper arm from underneath. "Certainly. Especially if there's cake involved."

Enjoying the warmth her touch on his arm caused, he followed Heidi through the crowd to the back of the house, saying hello to the guests, which included Phoebe's brother, Drew, her mom and dad, Grace and

Hugh, as well as Molly's fiancé, Grant, Mrs. Philpot and, of course, Heidi's co-conspirators, Lily and Molly.

As they stepped out onto the balloon-adorned deck, Heidi ran forward with colorful party hats in her hands. "Here, put these on."

Phoebe gave him an amused look as she took her hat and set it on her head, securing it underneath her chin with the elastic. "I'm going to have hat hair."

He put his on, deliberately setting it at a goofy angle on his head so it stuck out sideways. "You'll look great, hat hair or not."

Laughing, she said, "You ought to reserve judgment. Curly hair doesn't look good flat. Or not flat. You should see me in the morning."

"I'm sure you look great," he said truthfully, slipping his arm around her shoulder as if it was the most natural thing in the world.

"What I look is scary," she said, moving closer and then winding her arm around his back. "I've been known to frighten small children who see me before I have a chance to get my hair under control."

He squeezed her shoulder, savoring her closeness. "I can't imagine you scaring anybody." Although, the emotions she stirred in him *were* pretty terrifying.

Her reply was precluded by a beaming Heidi walking toward them, a crooked birthday cake decorated with loads of chocolate frosting, multicolored sprinkles and blazing birthday candles gripped tightly in her hands.

Someone started to sing "Happy Birthday," and everyone joined in, most off tune. Carson sang along as Phoebe's arm tightened around him, and he pulled her closer, looking down at her. She turned and gazed right at him, her mouth pressed up into a truly radiant smile that made his knees go weak. Her stunning eyes sparkled with what looked like distinct delight.

The song ended, and Heidi said, "Blow out the candles!" She held the cake up high. "And don't forget to make a wish."

Phoebe unwound her arm from around him and, nodding, leaned forward, holding her hair back with one hand. She took a deep breath and then blew, and all the candles went out. The guests cheered, and she straightened and turned, knocking him flat with another luminous smile.

"What did you wish for?" he asked, stunned that a woman with a silly cardboard birthday hat on her head could look so beautiful.

"If I tell you, it won't come true," she said, lifting a delicate eyebrow.

"Can you just give me a hint?" What would he say if she told him her wish had something to do with him? And Heidi? And the three of them being a family?

Whoa. Pretty big thoughts there. Life-altering, actually. But undeniable, nonetheless.

Before she could reply, Heidi gestured toward the picnic table with her chin. "You want to help me cut the cake?" she said to Phoebe.

"Of course." Phoebe put her arm around Heidi's shoulder, then turned to him. "Cake-cutting duty calls."

"Cut me an extrabig piece," he said, holding his hands a foot apart.

"Dad, that would mean you get the whole cake."

"Your point?" he said, teasing.

Heidi gave him an exasperated look. "I made one cake, so you only get your share."

"Well, since you made it, I'm going to at least want seconds," he said. "And thirds."

Heidi made oinking sounds.

Grinning, he watched her and Phoebe head over to the picnic table, his gaze lingering on their blond heads close together.

Phoebe and his daughter had obviously bonded over the past week. His heart warmed, and something akin to tenderness seeped through him; Phoebe was clearly a good influence on Heidi, and he was pretty sure she'd be in his daughter's life no matter what.

The question was, did he want her in *his* life on a more permanent basis, as more than just the kind woman in town who had befriended his daughter? Could he open his heart fully to Phoebe, and if he somehow found the will and courage to do so, would she return his feelings? Or would she cut him off, causing even more heartache than he'd have to deal with if he just went along as he always did, minimizing emotional turmoil by keeping his heart wrapped in barbed wire?

He put his hands on his hips and looked at the darkening sky. He couldn't remember the last time he'd faced such a chancy predicament.

Maybe, just maybe, he'd have to take a very smart woman's advice and ask God for some help with his dilemma.

Hovering near the picnic table, Phoebe tried not to stare at Carson as he talked to Grant on the other side of the deck. Instead she eyed the cake, seriously considering another piece of chocolate decadence.

Was she simply trading one indulgence for another, though?

She heard Carson laugh, and her gaze was again drawn his way. Boy, he looked handsome tonight in his navy blue uniform, all broad-shouldered, clean-cut and hero-ish, as if he could take on any burden thrown at him and look mighty fine doing it.

She reached out and straightened the plastic knives and forks on the table and made sure the paper napkins were in a neat pile and placed just so.

She'd been beyond stunned when she'd walked into Carson's house to her very own surprise birthday party, especially since her birthday wasn't until Monday.

Despite her shock, she'd been pleased. It meant a lot to her that Carson and Heidi, with Lily and Molly along for the ride, had taken the time to plan this party for her. The group effort made her feel special. Cherished. Well thought of.

Those feelings, in turn, had softened her heart until if felt like a ball of goo clogging up her chest. But instead of wanting to run away from what was going on inside and shore up her defenses by forcing starch into her heart, she felt the urge to throw herself into Carson's strong arms, kiss him silly and then drag Heidi into the cozy circle and beg to be part of this wonderful family.

She cast another surreptitious glance toward Carson and Grant, chewing on her lip. No doubt about it. She had a bad case of the love bug, times two. And, as usual, she didn't quite know what to do about finding a cure for the illness.

"I'm getting the sense you kind of like him."

Phoebe whipped her gaze around and saw Lily standing next to her, her brow raised in blatant speculation.

"Kind of? Ha!" Phoebe said without thinking. And, boy, oh, boy, Carson's attractiveness was about so much more than just his fantastic good looks. He had the charm and emotional appeal to back up the Really Good Guy persona, no problem.

Lily blinked, then moved over and cut herself a piece of cake. "Wow. I didn't expect such honesty."

"Yeah, well, I've been lying to myself for a while. Guess I'm getting tired of it." She'd come a long way. Far enough, though, to jump off an emotional cliff and risk her heart? That was the million dollar, seemingly unanswerable, question. "I guess I really don't know what's going on."

"I sense some…conflict," Lily said after she took a bite of cake. "Care to talk?"

Phoebe sighed, then rubbed the bridge of her nose and resisted the impulse to straighten the plastic cups sitting next to the punch on the table. "Maybe I do need some advice."

"Shoot."

"Well…" Phoebe cast another baleful gaze at Carson. Her heart fluttered. "I think I might have a… thing for your cousin."

Lily didn't bat an eye. "And?"

"And…that scares me to death."

"Why?" Lily asked, stabbing her fork in Phoebe's direction.

Phoebe frowned. "You call this talking, giving me nothing but one-word questions?" She snorted. "How about some answers."

Lily scraped a bit of frosting from her plate, then shrugged. "Sorry, but I don't have any pat answers."

"Yeah, me, neither," Phoebe replied glumly.

"But I do have some questions."

"Fire away." Phoebe was desperate enough to open up any line of questioning. What was the saying? Only the strong survived? She was going to do her best to be bulletproof.

"Okay." Lily set her plate down, then turned serious brown eyes to Phoebe. "Actually, I only have one question."

Phoebe nodded as if to say, *and what is it?*

"Do you love Carson, and do you love Heidi?"

Phoebe froze, her insides shuddering under the heavy dose of reality Lily was heaping on her.

Lily held her hand out.

Shaking, Phoebe took it, as if Lily's grasp was a lifeline on a fast-sinking ship.

"Because if the answer is yes, then in my book, if you want to be happy, you need to take a gamble and tell him, or risk losing a wonderful chance to find happiness with one of the best men you're ever going to meet."

"I was afraid you were going to say that," Phoebe said. Looked as if she had her path laid out.

She only wished she had an idea whether her final destination was the magical town of Happily Ever After or the dismal city of Heartbreak, Part Two.

Chapter Fourteen

"So, what's going on between you and my dad?"

Phoebe almost choked on the water she was sipping. She managed to swallow, then looked at Heidi standing by the small copier in Phoebe's office. "Um...what do you mean?" she shoved out, stalling, because she knew exactly what Heidi meant but didn't want to deal with the answer.

Heidi pushed the green Print button on the copier. "Well, do you guys like each other, or what?" The copier whirred into action, spitting out the bright yellow flyers touting their monthly ice cream special.

Tricky question. Two days had passed since Phoebe's birthday party at the Winterses', and though she and Carson hadn't spent any time together alone, he had stopped by for a cone yesterday, which in itself would have been a rather innocuous occurrence. Though, she'd enjoyed indulging in giant cones with him and Heidi out on one of the wooden benches lining the boardwalk.

But when he'd stopped to talk to elderly Mrs. Lerman, who'd toddled into the parlor with her grandkids for sundaes, and offered to repair the window in her house that some raucous kids had vandalized the night before, Phoebe's insides had gone ooey-gooey again, and her heart had melted faster than the cone in her hand. It was no overstatement to say that she'd totally understood the look of utter adoration Mrs. Lerman had nailed him with.

Times five. Hundred.

If that wasn't an undeniable indication of her true feelings, she'd eat the box of straws on the counter and ask for another serving.

And now, here Heidi was, asking a loaded question, trying to pin Phoebe down.

Phoebe would like nothing more than to tell Heidi she was falling for her dad, and that Phoebe had decided last night after another heartfelt conversation with God that she was willing to go out on an emotional limb and tell Carson how she felt. Soon.

But that was between her and him, and it wouldn't be right to fill Heidi in before she told Carson that she wanted to take their relationship to the next level. So rather than state the exact truth, instead she said, "Well, sure, I like your dad, honey. He's very nice." More than nice. Perfect, actually.

"But do you *like* him?" Heidi asked with a pointed look.

Hoo, boy. Nothing like a hopeful preteen trying to nail you down on romantic details. Phoebe was going o have to finesse her way through this conversation, for sure. "As in do I want to be his girlfriend?"

"Yeah," Heidi said as she gathered the pile of flyers off the tray of the copier. "Like that."

"Um...well, I'm not sure your dad is looking for a girlfriend."

"Well, he should be," Heidi said with twelve-year-old conviction. "Especially if it'd be you."

"Why do you say that?" Phoebe asked, casually straightening some papers on her desk. Call her needy, but denying an itty-bitty ego stroke from Heidi wasn't happening.

"'Cause you're the best," Heidi announced with a shrug of her shoulders, as if the answer was obvious. "And I think he really likes you."

Phoebe's tummy dropped. "What do you mean?" she asked, striving to keep her voice laid-back, even though her desire to hear about why Heidi thought Carson liked her was anything but casual. "Did he say something to you?"

"No, he didn't say anything. But I can just tell by the way he looks at you that he likes you."

"How's that?" Phoebe asked, her voice high, realizing as she said the words that she sounded like a curious parrot.

"Oh, you know, how Prince Charming looked at Cinderella." Heidi made a funny face. "All googly-eyed."

Phoebe laughed, then let Heidi's proclamation sink

in. When it did, she couldn't deny the giddy feelings darting through her.

One more reason Phoebe was even more sure of the path she'd set out last night after praying for guidance. Now she definitely had to go to the next stage of her relationship with Carson. She had to tell him how she felt. And she had to answer Heidi.

Rising, she went over and took the flyers from her. "While I appreciate your observations, at the moment there is nothing going on between me and your dad." But perhaps soon, there would be...

Heidi's face fell. "Do you think something might happen...someday?"

Phoebe set the flyers down and made her expression soft and understanding. "I honestly can't say, sweetie." Although it sure would make things easier if she could flip to the end of the book and read the ending of the story of her and Carson.

"But there's a chance, right?" Heidi asked, her voice rife with possibility.

Phoebe couldn't lie. "Maybe."

Heidi clapped her hands.

"But I'm not promising anything, all right?"

Her eyes glowing, Heidi said, "All right."

Just then, the phone on Phoebe's desk rang. She picked up the receiver. "I Scream for Ice Cream, Phoebe speaking. How may I help you."

"Phoebe, it's Carson."

Her heart thudded at the sound of his voice. "Hey

Do you need to talk to Heidi?" She pointed to the phone and mouthed to Heidi, "It's your dad."

"No." A significant pause. "Um…I had an accident while on a call at work, and I'm at the E.R."

Emergency room? The bottom fell out of her stomach. Oh, no. Not again. She'd heard those ominous words before. "Okay…" she pushed out, struggling to stay calm when her gut was in an instant knot, keeping her response neutral for Heidi's benefit.

"I was wondering if you could take care of Heidi for the afternoon," he asked, his voice strained and clearly tinged with pain. "Mrs. P. had a doctor's appointment, and I was supposed to go home early, but I'm not going to be able to leave here for a while."

Phoebe's instincts had her saying, "I'm coming down there."

"No, I need you to take care of Heidi."

Phoebe closed her eyes and bit her lip, imposing a poise into her voice that didn't exist. "Can you fill me in?" she asked evenly, dreading his answer, yet having to ask for her own sanity.

A muffled voice sounded in the background. Another pause. "I have to go now," he said gruffly. "The doctor's back. Please just hang on to Heidi, tell her everything is going to be fine, and I'll call as soon as I know more."

Everything in Phoebe screamed for more information, to demand details to soothe her own fears; this situation held a heartrending echo of the past she'd never wanted to hear again.

"O-okay," she replied, managing somehow to erase the stress from her voice for Carson's sake. He needed her to be calm under fire, even though panic chomped at her composure like a shark demolishing its prey. "Don't worry about us, we'll be fine."

"Thanks," he replied. "I'll be in touch." And then the line clicked dead.

Phoebe hung up, sending out silent prayer. *God, I really need You now. Please take care of Carson.*

Feeling slightly calmer from her prayer, she looked at Heidi.

"What did my dad want?" Heidi asked.

By sheer dint of will, Phoebe plastered an unruffled expression on her face, deciding on the fly that she could not lie to Heidi; she'd eventually find out the truth and would surely figure out that Phoebe had tried to sugarcoat or deny the situation.

"Um…he's had a minor accident and had to get checked out at the hospital."

Alarm blossomed on Heidi's face.

Phoebe held up a hand. "He's going to be fine, so don't worry." She forced a smile, trying to take her own advice and failing miserably. "And you get to spend the rest of the day with me."

"What happened?" Heidi asked, wide-eyed.

"The doctor was there, and your dad couldn't go into details," Phoebe replied, amazed at how calm she sounded when worry was riding her so hard her heart felt as if it were going to explode. "He'll call me when he has time."

After a hesitation, Heidi said, "Maybe we should go to the hospital."

Phoebe understood the response—she'd had the same reactionary instinct just moments ago—but the rational part of her told her that the last thing Heidi needed was to spend hours hanging around the E.R. Especially if something went wrong....

Phoebe suppressed little squeak of half fear, half worry, and forced a calm demeanor worthy of an Oscar, if she did say so herself. "Nah, he said everything is going to be fine, and I think so, too. So why don't we finish up those flyers, and then how about lunch as soon as Tanya gets here?"

Heidi nodded, her eyes reflecting the same panicky emotions churning through Phoebe. "I'm not very hungry," she said, her words contradicting her nod.

"Yeah, me, neither." Not with this rock of lumpy anxiety lodged painfully in her gut. "So how about we keep busy here, and I'm sure we'll hear from your dad real soon."

Heidi's eyes glimmered. "Phoebe, I'm scared."

Her eyes burning, Phoebe went over and hugged Heidi. "That's natural," she said. "But your dad's tough, and if it were something really serious, he wouldn't have been able to call me, correct?" Phoebe hung on to that thought with everything in her.

Heidi sucked in a shuddering breath.

"So hang tight. Don't jump the gun and assume the worst, all right?" Phoebe said.

Nodding against her shoulder, Heidi replied, "Okay."

Phoebe had said all the right things, soothed Heidi as best she could. Even so, she wished she could believe her own rationale. But the truth was, she didn't. She knew from tragic experience that bad things happened to good people. That loved ones could be taken away in a heartbeat. And that dire phone calls could lead to heartbreak.

A hair-raising realization followed on the heels of those thoughts: What was she going to do if Carson wasn't okay?

And how could she possibly take their relationship to the next level now that he'd proved himself to be just as likely as Justin had been to be put in harm's way because of his job?

As dread sunk its talons into her, she decided that it was definitely time to go back to protecting her heart.

After an endless afternoon in the E.R., being subjected to pokes, prods and finally X-rays, Carson was beyond glad to be home.

Turns out he'd fractured his left ankle when he carelessly stepped in a pothole while helping two elderly men, Neil and Floyd, who'd backed their boat off a landing into Moonlight Cove Lake. Talk about a silly accident. Wait till the guys at the station got a load of what had happened. They'd never let him hear the end of how he'd been injured on such a routine call.

Shaking his head at his own stupidity, he threw open the door of Phoebe's small car, then waited for

ner to come around and hand him the crutches she'd
stashed in the trunk.

His ankle throbbed with every beat of his heart, and
he wondered at the wisdom of refusing the pain meds
the E.R. doc had suggested. No, no. He could handle
the pain. Although, admittedly, he'd never broken a
bone before, either, and a busted ankle was going to be
more of a challenge to handle than the routine aches
and pains from sports and exercise he'd dealt with in
the past.

Her face noticeably pale, Phoebe came hurrying
around the back of the car, the crutches in hand. "Here
you go."

Carson grabbed them and lifted his casted lower
leg out of the car, then clumsily tried to situate the
crutches under his armpits, which was a trick in the
low car. Finally he succeeded in getting everything in
the right place. Taking a deep breath, he awkwardly
hoisted himself to his feet, hopping around on his
good ankle to find his balance. A wave of dizziness
crashed through him, and the ground tilted.

Phoebe stepped close and took his arm. "Hey, there.
Take it easy."

He clenched his jaw; if not for her steadying hold,
he probably would have toppled over like a felled tree.
"I'm fine."

"I know, but you've been through a trauma, and
your body needs some time to adjust."

Frustration pounded away at him. "I should be able

to handle crutches," he ground out, blinking to clear his wooziness.

"Yeah, well, just be thankful it was an ankle injury and not higher up on your leg." Phoebe took a better hold on his upper arm. "Drew broke his femur in two places when he fell off his bike as a kid, and he was in a wheelchair for weeks. I'd like to see you handle one of those babies."

Man, her hand on his arm felt good. Comforting. Warm. Soft.

Just what he needed.

He looked down at her, liking how the late-afternoon sun shined into her eyes, turning them into an almost translucent baby blue. "You wanna follow me for the next six weeks with that arm around me just in case? At least something good would come of this stupid injury."

She rolled her eyes, but her cheeks got rosier. "Stop, will you? You're being silly."

He shook his head and immediately regretted the sharp motion. "Maybe, but having you by my side all the time sounds pretty good." Especially after he'd prayed last night about how to handle his feelings for Phoebe and had actually come away with answers. With God's help, he was getting past some of his fears.

She stiffened noticeably, her shoulders raising a bit, but she didn't comment. He looked down, and she seemed to be studiously ignoring his gaze. Her delicate jaw was taut beneath the fall of her curly hair.

He came to an awkward halt. "Hey," he said, jump

ing in place a bit on his good leg to stay balanced. "Is something wrong?"

Turning her gaze up, she pressed her mouth into a bright smile that appeared completely fake. Totally put-on for his benefit. "What? No."

He scoffed. "I might have broken my leg, but my brain isn't busted. Something's bothering you."

After a long pause, she nodded. "It's just been a stressful day, is all," she said, avoiding his gaze as she pulled slightly on him to get him moving.

He resisted her urging. "Phoebe, talk to me." Her distance, which he'd picked up on when she'd shown up to get him at the hospital, bothered him. A lot. He'd become used to having her close, having her to lean on, and the thought of losing that nearness and support had his gut rolling.

She pressed her lips together, and something flashed in her eyes. Sadness? Or a bit of anger? Frustration? He wished he could tell, but he'd never been good at deciphering emotions.

Sighing, she said, "Carson, you broke your ankle today, and we're standing in your driveway while you're about to fall down. Can't we talk about this later?"

In answer, his ankle throbbed and the driveway lurched again. Despite the crutches under his arms, he involuntarily listed slightly away from her.

Phoebe dug her feet into the ground and grabbed on to him hard, pulling him straight. "See? You're in no condition to be standing out here talking."

Clearly, she was dodging the conversation. But she had a point; the E.R. doc had told him to keep his foot elevated for the next twenty-four hours, so he'd let her dodge away. For now. But one way or another, he'd figure out what was going on with her.

"You're right," he concurred, adjusting the crutches under himself more fully without putting any weight on his bum ankle. "But something's bothering you, and sooner or later you're going to have to tell me what it is."

She applied pressure to the small of his back, nudging him toward the front door. "I'm going to agree with you just so you'll drop the subject and get yourself into the house where you can put your foot up."

Her statement didn't sit right with him, and he opened his mouth to question her again. But his response was cut off when Heidi ran out of the house followed by Mrs. Philpot. He clamped his lips together, resigning himself to staying clueless—and worried—about Phoebe for a bit longer.

"Daddy!" Heidi cried, hustling off the porch toward him, her hair blowing wildly in the ever-present ocean breeze.

Phoebe stepped away, letting him stand on his own with the crutches for support.

Heidi stopped short of mowing him down, her gaze fastened on the navy blue cast encasing his ankle. "Oh, wow. Cool cast."

"Yeah, just the accessory I've always wanted," he said with a crooked smiled. "Goes with anything."

"I'm just glad you're okay," Heidi said, her eyes sparking with residual worry. "Phoebe and I were really worried when you called."

He gave Phoebe a questioning look. "Oh, really?"

She just stared back. Blank. Odd. Kind of Stepford-ish, actually. He slammed his eyebrows together. Who was this cardboard woman standing next to him? Not that he wanted her to worry unduly about him, of course. But some kind of reaction would set his mind at ease.

Mrs. Philpot arrived, as calm as ever, precluding any further private discussion with Phoebe. "Sheriff, glad to see you home."

"Thanks, Mrs. P."

She gestured into the house. "I'm sure the doctor wants you off your feet and resting, and I'm guessing you're starving. So I took the liberty of making you some soup and homemade bread for dinner."

His stomach growled, taking his mind off his injury—and Phoebe's weird remoteness—for a few welcome seconds. "Bless you, Mrs. P., for thinking of that."

"Let's get you inside," Phoebe said, her voice sounding carefully modulated, so very un-Phoebelike, confirming his suspicion that something was bothering her. Something big. "Doctor's orders, Sheriff Winters."

He allowed himself to be herded into the house by the three females determined to coddle him. He let them coddle away as he settled on the couch, his thoughts distracted by Phoebe's demeanor. Had something happened since her birthday party? Her attitude had done an about-face worthy of a military march since then.

Mrs. Philpot headed into the kitchen, and Heidi went off to find a pillow for his ankle. Wordlessly, Phoebe made to follow Mrs. Philpot.

"Phoebe?" he called out. He wasn't going to let her scurry off so easily.

She froze, then turned slowly, smoothing her hair back behind one ear. "Yes?"

"This conversation isn't done."

The line of her jaw hardened. "I know," she said, nodding.

Her response, while logical, sent a chill into his heart; clearly she had something to say. Eventually. "What's wrong?" he asked, giving it one more try.

"We'll talk later," she replied, a stubborn tilt to her chin. "Now isn't the time."

To accentuate that point, Mrs. Philpot came out with a tray in her hands. "Here you go, Sheriff. My special-recipe chicken noodle soup."

All he could do was nod at Phoebe as Mrs. Philpot set the tray on the coffee table.

"Thanks, Mrs. P. It looks delicious."

The next thing he knew, Phoebe had quietly disappeared into the kitchen, and his gut churned as worry set in. She was putting up a wall, shutting him out. Figured she'd pull away just when he wanted her closer.

Mrs. Philpot handed his soup bowl to him, but his appetite was suddenly nada. He took a bite anyway and made sounds of approval, even as a disconcerting thought dug its claws into him: Had he lost Phoebe before he'd figured things out enough to actually find her? That sobering realization hit him much harder than he'd ever expected.

And suddenly his heart felt even more broken than his ankle.

Chapter Fifteen

With her heart in her throat and the stiff breeze cooling her cheeks, Phoebe stood on the Winterses' doorstep the day after she'd driven Carson home from the hospital, dreading the conversation to come.

But there was no help for it, no avoiding the inevitable. After a long, sleepless night and many prayers to God, she'd decided what she had to do about Carson.

Her chest grew tight, forcing a wince.

She took a deep breath, lifted her hand and knocked, willing herself to stay, face him and tell him the truth. She owed him—and Heidi—that much.

A few moments later, he answered the door, his crutches tucked under each arm. He wore a blue T-shirt and athletic shorts—undoubtedly to accommodate his cast—and his hair was messy, as if he'd been jamming his fingers through it repeatedly.

Even so, he looked as handsome as ever with his shadowed jaw and dark coloring. Perfect, actually. Too bad that wasn't enough.

His mouth broke into a smile. "Phoebe! I didn't expect to see you."

"I guess I should have called." But then she might have chickened out.

"No, no." He used his crutches to back up. "Come in."

Thrusting her chin up for courage—no matter how false—she stepped inside and smoothed her hair down, fighting the urge to bolt. He shut the door with his left crutch, then deftly hobbled around her.

"You're getting pretty good with those things," she said, going for impersonal right off the bat, as if that might help her keep her heart out of saying what had to be said.

"Yeah, I'm getting the hang of it."

"Are you in pain?"

He lifted his broad shoulders. "Not really. Ibuprofen seems to be doing the trick."

"Good, good," she said inanely, hating the sound of the small talk she'd started, but at a loss as to how to approach the difficult discussion to come.

"Phoebe, why are you here?" he asked after a long silence.

She cleared her throat. "Can we go sit?" She nodded to the leather couch in the living room.

"Sure." He pointed left with his crutch. "After you."

Hitching her purse up on her shoulder, she walked to the sofa and sat down, holding her back ramrod straight.

Carson made his way over, then set his crutches

on the floor. Nimbly he hopped the last little bit and
eased himself down next to her.

He smelled like laundry detergent and man, so she
tried not to breathe.

Turning to face her, he put an arm on the top of the
couch behind her. "You gonna put your purse down
and stay awhile?" he asked with a lift of one brow.

Her cheeks heated. "Oh, yeah." She set the bag
down at her feet, then clasped her hands tightly together in her lap.

"I take it you want to continue the conversation we
started yesterday," he said matter-of-factly.

"What makes you think that?" she said before she
realized how ridiculous the question sounded.

"Lucky guess. You seem mighty uncomfortable."

"I do?" Why did he have to be so perceptive? Although, she was sure her body language spoke volumes.

"Yep. You look like you're going to bolt." He
glanced down. "And like you're going to squeeze the
life out of your own hands any second now."

Unclenching her knotted fingers, she forced her
spine to relax a bit, to alter her body language enough
to present a serene front.

"Sorry." She stared at her toes and fought the urge
to straighten the cuffs on her roll-up capris. "Guess I
am a bit stressed out."

Patiently, he waited for her to go on. Words stuck
in her throat, though. How was she going to do this,

to herself and to him? Maybe she'd made a mistake by coming here...

"Phoebe, haven't we always been honest with each other?"

She nodded. "Yes."

"So why stop now? You've obviously got something on your mind. With all due respect, I would hope you think enough of me to let me in on what's going through that pretty head of yours."

Good point. In fact, she wished she didn't think so highly of him; telling him about her decision would be easier if she didn't care about him and his daughter so much.

"You're right," she said, turning to give him her full attention, forcing herself to look right at those compelling dark eyes. "So, at my birthday party, I talked to Lily, and I really thought maybe you and I...had some kind of future together."

He took her hand, burning her skin where he touched her. "I do, too."

His words took her off guard, and something melted inside of her. "You do?"

"Yep. I saw you with Heidi, and something clicked."

Her chest started burning. "I didn't know that," she said. But even if she had known, would it have changed anything? His point was moot now; she'd made her choice, and there was no turning back.

"That's because you shut me out last night when you brought me home, and I didn't have a chance to tell you." He brought up her hand and kissed her knuckles. "Sometimes you miss important things when you clam up."

Regret for putting him off burned through her, but the touch of his lips on her hand literally seared her. "I see that now," she managed. "I...guess I just wasn't ready to talk."

"But you're ready now, right?" He squeezed her hand. "Because I have some things I want to say, too."

She should have known this wouldn't be a one-way conversation. "You do?"

"Of course."

She blinked.

"What?" He gave her a tilted smile. "You think you're the only one who's been doing some thinking about the two of us?"

The two of us. She liked the sound of that...no, no, she didn't. There was no *us,* and never would be. Not now that she'd survived another harrowing scare, believing something terrible had happened to the man she'd thought she could let herself love.

"Of course not," she said weakly.

"I thought we said we were going for honesty," he replied, his voice gentle and devoid of reproach.

"Yes." She pulled her hand away from him so she could think clearly. The loss of his touch hollowed her out, made her feel raw inside. "Honesty is the theme of the day."

He looked at her expectantly. "You go first."

First. Wonderful.

She drew in a deep breath and tried to ignore her

bleeding insides. The time had come for her to tell him goodbye. To do the right thing. To protect her heart once and for all from loss, without looking back or letting herself be a foolish slave to possible regrets.

Except…funny how doing the right thing, *the only thing,* felt so completely and utterly wrong.

Carson saw Phoebe suck in that shaky breath, as if she were bracing herself for something bad. Something that might break his heart?

He shifted on the couch, preparing himself for whatever she was going to lay on him. He'd let her say her piece, and then deal. Isn't that what he always did? Buck up and handle life's bullets?

"So," she said. "When you called me yesterday to tell me you were in the hospital, it brought back a lot of memories of another call I received telling me someone I cared about was in the hospital."

He froze as jagged realization jolted through him. "Your fiancé."

"Yes," she said in an overly even voice. As if she were holding on to her composure by a thread and had to compensate, but went too far and sounded like a robot instead of a person. Who could blame her, given the tragic subject matter?

"Oh, man." He raked a hand through his hair. "I should have realized."

"No, you're not responsible for taking care of me."

"I'd like to be," he said before he could call back the words.

After a blink and a pause, she held up a rigid hand. "Don't distract me from what I have to say."

He inclined his head in agreement.

"Justin lived for a short time after he got caught in the wildfire."

Horror shot through Carson, dark and awful. He nodded for her to go on; if she could deal with talking about this, then he'd listen all night if necessary.

"His parents and I drove overnight to the hospital in Bend, Oregon, where they took him after the accident." Her lips trembled and her eyes watered. "He died before we could get there."

He reached for her hand, but she waved him off. "No, let me finish. So when you called, memories of that day came back, and I was so, so scared." She pressed a hand to her mouth, then continued. "And I realized that I can't set myself up to care for someone, only to have that person yanked away from me."

"But I'm fine," he said, spreading his arms wide, then gesturing to his cast. "I hurt myself stepping in a pothole. This thing will be history in six weeks, and then I'll be as good as new."

"Next time might be another story."

He shook his head. "There won't be a next time," he replied, trying to stay calm when everything within him screamed to shake her and tell her that her reasoning was flawed. Wrong.

"You're a cop, Carson."

"In Moonlight Cove," he replied, scoffing. "Hardly a hotbed of dangerous criminal activity."

"You're splitting hairs," she said.

"No, I'm being realistic."

"And I am, too. My fears are real. Feelings are feelings, so your point is moot."

He looked at her helplessly; this conversation was getting away from him, and he had no idea what to do about it. "What are you saying?"

"That no matter what, I won't let there be a next time," she said in a voice rife with determination.

A chill ran through him. "What do you mean, exactly?"

"I could have fallen in love with you, Carson," she said, her voice breaking.

His hopes soared and his heart squeezed.

Tears crested and tumbled onto her pale cheeks. "But after what happened, after I got your call, I realized I have to stop myself from falling completely in love *now,* before I'm in so deep I can't walk away without ripping out my own heart, and before losing you one way or another would completely devastate me."

Echoes of Susan's desertion reverberated through him. "This conversation is familiar," he said, feeling as if he'd been knifed in the heart. "Too familiar."

Phoebe blinked, then whispered, "Your ex-wife?"

He nodded crisply once.

"You've never told me what happened."

By design. Maybe that was his problem. Too little too late, probably. But he sensed he needed to heed the lesson being shoved on him, even if he dreaded the subject matter.

He let out a weighty breath, then awkwardly stood and hobbled over on his crutches to look out the front window, noting the gray clouds moving in. Then he opened his mouth and forced himself to reveal his greatest failing and most profound shame. "Susan blamed me for CJ's death," he admitted. "Said it was my fault and that she wouldn't ever be able to forgive me."

Silence.

He went on. "She couldn't deal with it, refused to, actually, even for Heidi's sake."

A tiny gasp.

"So one day, she got up, packed a suitcase and left without saying goodbye to either me or Heidi, just like that," he said, snapping his fingers. "I felt like she'd hit me over the head with a two-by-four."

After another beat of quiet, Phoebe sniffed, then said, "Carson, I'm so sorry. The way she left was terrible. Obviously she was so caught up in her grief she wasn't thinking straight."

He swung around. "You're defending her?"

With a lift to her chin, Phoebe stood and said, "Yes, I am, because she lost a child, too, and her heart was broken just as yours was."

She drew in a shuddering breath. "I know how awful that feels, to lose someone you love and have your heart hurt so much you don't think you'll survive." Shaking her head, her eyes shimmering, she added, "I was so crazy with grief, I thought of doing all kinds of stupid things in the months after Justin died."

Her point hit home, and his heart swelled with emotions he refused to name; this was one incredible woman here, and he wished he could take away the shadows of her grief and pain. But he couldn't.

But he *could* recognize the validity of her statement, which might allow him to see Susan's heartbreak through fresh eyes.

Phoebe's eyes.

Somehow, he felt as if some of the burden he'd been carrying lifted slightly, as if her thoughts would, ultimately, help him forgive Susan for her desertion, and maybe even forgive himself for CJ's death. Bless Phoebe for that amazing gift. "I guess I never thought of it that way," he replied.

"I'm not saying what she did was right, but I understand."

"I guess I understand a bit more, too." He reached out and took her hand. "Thank you for that."

She squeezed his hand. "You have got to find a way to forgive yourself for your son's death, Carson. If you don't, the guilt will eat you up and take over your life."

Again, her thoughts made a lot of sense. His guilt had taken over, and he saw now he never should have allowed it.

Phoebe spoke again. "So you understand why I have to end this?"

He backtracked on their conversation, recalling his

point. "I get it, trust me. But I still think you're jumping to a conclusion that isn't valid."

"You're a cop—"

"And you're using my job as an excuse."

She drew her chin in sharply. "I am not."

"Yes, you are, and here's why—"

"Why *you* think why," she shot back, cutting him off again, crossing her arms over her chest, clearly gearing up for a fight.

Fine. He'd enter the bout. A lot was at stake—more than he'd realized—and he wouldn't just bow out without fighting a good battle. No way. "Granted. But I happen to think my statement is true. You're scared to love me, so you're using my job as an excuse to avoid your feelings."

"You're wrong," she said, her face tight. Expressionless.

Grabbing on to that, he said, "Look at you. Your face says it all."

She stepped away, putting the coffee table between them. "What do you mean?"

He instinctively followed, stumbling when he automatically put weight on his bum ankle. "Ow!" he exclaimed, hopping onto his good leg before he leaned on his crutches, taking weight off his bad ankle. "So, as I was saying, your face is like a mask, hiding everything you're feeling."

She looked stricken, then recovered. "Well, if it is, it's certainly not intentional."

"That's even more telling," he said. "Your subconscious is at work, telling you to cover up to protect yourself."

"Okay, fine." She lifted her chin. "So I'm covering up. The end result is the same. To protect myself, I have to tell you goodbye," she said, picking up her purse from the floor and slinging it over her shoulder.

Goodbye. Wow. It sounded so final. So wrong. So not what he wanted. There was no way he could ignore that feeling.

He maneuvered himself around the coffee table, then used his crutches to take him over so he was standing right in front of her. Her chin fell and she looked away. More hiding.

He used his finger to force her to look at him. "Tell me to my face goodbye is what you really want."

Her mouth worked, and she tried to look away again.

"Nope," he said, pressing her chin in his direction. "If you really want to do this, you're going to have to look at me and say it."

Complying with the push of his hand, she turned and looked at him, her blue eyes shimmering with more tears. "This…goodbye…is what I really want," she whispered hoarsely. "Please don't make it any harder than it already is."

His gut clenched. "Okay, then. I won't fight you on this. I can't force you to stay." True enough, though it was tempting to lock and bar the doors to keep her here.

She wiped her eyes, then nodded. "Thank you. Can you please tell Heidi that I'd still like her to help me out at the store?"

"Of course," he said.

She drew in a shaky breath, then visibly hardened her jaw. "I'm truly sorry for this."

A nod was all he could give. Anything more and he'd probably break down, at least on the inside. Good thing he was adept at making the outside look impenetrable.

After a beat of silence, she turned and walked away. Out of his house. Out of his life.

But never, he feared, out of his heart.

Chapter Sixteen

"Are you all right, Phoebe? You don't look so good."

Phoebe looked at Tanya as she set her purse on the counter. "I'm fine," she said, trying to infuse some super-duper happy fineness into her voice. But she wasn't fine at all. In fact, she was terrible.

Saying goodbye to Carson was the hardest thing she'd ever had to do. Ironic, wasn't it? She was supposed to be avoiding pain, protecting herself from this kind of heartbreak by shoving Carson away. And yet here she was, feeling as if she'd eviscerated herself with a dull knife.

"You sure?" Tanya asked with a furrowed brow, coming nearer. "There's a nasty flu going around..."

Unless it was the heart flu, that wasn't what Phoebe suffered from. "I'm just tired," Phoebe said as she straightened the napkin holders, tucking the stray napkins into their place. A teensy stretch, yes. But the last thing she wanted to do was drag an employee into her romantic problems. And she *was* tired; she hadn't had a good night's sleep for quite a while.

"You want to go home and rest?" Tanya asked. "I can hold down the fort here."

Phoebe waved a hand in the air. "Nah, I'm fine. Once I get working, I'll get a second wind." And she needed to stay busy to keep her mind off Carson. Guess she'd be working for the rest of her life.

"You sure?" Tanya asked.

"Positive." Phoebe headed to her office as the doorbells sounded and some customers came in, bringing the briny smell of the ocean with them. "I'm going to work back here on accounts payable for a while. Let me know if things get busy and you need help."

"Okay."

When Phoebe got to her office, she flopped down in her desk chair, recalling the stricken expression on Carson's face when she'd told him that she had to say goodbye. She'd almost broken down then, especially when he'd talked about his wife walking out, and it had taken all of her mental fortitude to keep from throwing herself into his arms and telling him she'd made a big mistake.

But she hadn't made a mistake, she was sure of it. She'd spoken the absolute truth when she'd told Carson about the numbing fear she'd felt when she'd found out about his injury. No matter what, she had to make sure she never set herself up for heartbreak.

Although it seemed as if her heart was crumbling into itty-bitty pieces right now.

Right on cue, her eyes started burning. She pinched the bridge of her nose; she *would not* cry over Carson. She'd survive this, one way or another, with lots of work and backbone and determination. And one day, she'd look back with her calm protected life all arranged and safe and predictable, and she'd know she'd done what she had to minimize emotional trauma. End of story.

And, hopefully, she'd be happy. But she had her doubts. So be it. Everything had a price.

She only hoped letting Carson go wouldn't cost more than she could afford.

Three days after Phoebe said adios to him, Lily showed up at Carson's house out of the blue while he was trying to do paperwork with his leg propped up on the couch. The key word being *trying.* As in, thinking of anything but Phoebe.

"Hey, cuz," Lily said, waving, bringing the scent of the windy, rainy day in with her.

"Don't you knock?" he said, looking up with an eyebrow raised.

She dropped her purse on the recliner. "I didn't want you to have to get up."

"Okay, thanks." He shifted, trying to get comfortable, which was almost impossible with his cast. Thankfully, the doctor had cleared him for a walking boot in a week or so, and then he'd be back at work. At his desk. Doing more boring paperwork until he was healed.

Better than sitting around here, thinking about Phoebe. Although he doubted a change of scenery would erase her from his thoughts. He feared nothing would do that.

"So," Lily said pointedly. "What's up with you and Phoebe?" Aha. The reason for Lily's "impromptu" visit.

"Why do you ask?" he said, trying to stay smooth and nonchalant, in case Lily actually had no idea that Phoebe had essentially dumped him.

"Because Tanya told me Phoebe has been moping around the ice cream parlor, and that every time Tanya tries to find out what's wrong, Phoebe shuts the conversation down, claims to be under the weather and disappears into her office for hours on end."

Concern bubbled through him. "Is she sick?" he asked, sitting up straighter.

"*Love*sick, maybe," Lily shot back, staring him down. "Because of you?"

Was it possible Phoebe was mourning the death of their relationship, such as it was, as much has he'd been?

Suddenly, the thought of keeping his sadness hidden as he'd been doing in front of Heidi for days just didn't seem possible. He felt as if his heart had been replaced by a rock, and the odd combination of pain and emptiness had him blurting, "She called it quits, not the other way around."

Lily's face softened. "Oh, Carson, I'm so sorry."

"Yeah, me, too," he said truthfully. "I think she's running scared."

"Phoebe called it quits?" Heidi cried from the entry into the living room. "When?"

Carson closed his eyes, chiding himself for not being more careful. He'd been going to tell Heidi about Phoebe and him, but hadn't found the right time. Now she knew, and he had some explaining to do.

Lily went over and put a comforting arm around Heidi, then looked at him, her chin down. "You didn't tell her?"

"No, he didn't," Heidi said before he could reply. "He never tells me anything."

"I wasn't sure how to explain," he said, and the words sounded lame, lame, lame.

"You never want to talk about this kind of stuff," Heidi said with a frown. "I think you're just making an excuse."

Her statement hit a bull's-eye.

"For the record, I think so, too," Lily said.

They stood there staring at him, and he knew if Phoebe was here, she'd be shooting darts at him with her eyes, too.

Phoebe. If there was one thing he'd learned since he'd met her, it was the value of opening up, talking. Admitting his weaknesses. Letting himself be vulnerable without feeling like a weakling.

"You're right," he shoved out in her honor. "I have been making excuses." He patted the couch next to him. "Come on over here, honey, and sit down, and I'll tell you about what happened with Phoebe."

Heidi stomped over and plopped down next to him.

Lily regarded him, her arms crossed over her chest. "I'm not quite sure what's going on with you and Phoebe, but I can say that if you let that woman walk out on you without a huge fight, you've made a big mistake."

"You think I don't know that?" he said. "But she's pretty stubborn—"

"And you aren't?" Lily said.

He just stared at her.

"Enough said." Lily picked up her purse and pointed at him. "We still need to talk, but I'm going to let you two hash this out by yourselves." She looked at Heidi. "We still on for the movie this weekend?"

"Yeah," Heidi said.

"Okay, I'll see you guys later."

She left, and Carson turned and looked at his daughter. She regarded him, her mouth pressed downward and her eyes shining with what seemed to be an accusatory light.

Clearly, she thought he'd betrayed her. And in a way, he had. He should have leveled with her sooner. Man, he was still bad at this communication stuff.

"So what happened?" she asked. "Phoebe didn't say anything to me about this when I was working at the parlor yesterday."

"We had a long talk and decided that dating wasn't the right thing for us right now." There. Sounded reasonable enough, even though he didn't necessarily agree with the statement.

Heidi narrowed her eyes. "You said she called it quits."

He gave himself another mental head slap; not much got past this kid. "We decided together," he amended; no way was he going to lay the blame at Phoebe's feet. Heidi thought Phoebe could do no wrong, and he wasn't about to tarnish that notion in his daughter's eyes.

Heidi jumped up. "And she left?"

"Yes."

"Why didn't you stop her?"

"How was I supposed to do that? She's a grown-up, honey."

"Did you tell her you love her?"

His neck burned. "Well…no—"

"Why not?" Heidi cried. "If you had, she would have stayed."

Words stuck in his throat; she was, quite possibly, right. But maybe she was wrong…

Why didn't he have a clue, anyway? His feelings were so jumbled, so messed up, he wasn't sure what he felt.

Except for a big hole in his heart.

Fat tears formed in Heidi's eyes. "I can't believe you let her leave without telling her the truth."

The truth…

Before he could conjure up a response, Heidi said,

"Mom left, and now Phoebe's gone, and none of i is fair!"

Her words decimated him. "You're right, honey. none of this is fair. But your mom and Phoebe are two different people—"

"But they both left me," she said as tears ran dowr her cheeks. "Why did they leave me?"

"Their leaving had nothing to do with you, Heidi Nothing at all. So don't blame yourself for what's happened." He was the one at fault in Phoebe's case. He should have fought harder for her.

He tried to stand, but his cast hindered him and put him off-balance onto his bad ankle. Pain shot up his leg, and he staggered and then fell back onto the couch.

Heidi sobbed, then wheeled around at a run.

"Heidi, wait!" he called, trying to get to his feet again.

But she didn't heed his call, and within seconds she'd flown out the front door, leaving it open in her wake.

And then she was gone, and he was stuck with a bum leg and crutches, not to mention his mixed-up, skewed thinking that had probably cost him the woman he loved. And maybe his daughter, too.

On the third day after she said goodbye to Carson, Phoebe kept herself hidden in the back room working on supply ordering, feeling out of sorts and in a major funk.

She rubbed her brow, then put a hand on the aching spot over her heart. Was this how it was going to be, behaving like a hermit in her office, hiding from a life that seemed so much less happy now that Carson wasn't in it?

Wow. Depressing prospect for her future, for sure. But necessary to protect herself.

Feeling as if she had been hollowed out with an ice cream scoop, she booted up her computer, preparing to bury herself in revamping her marketing plan for the next year. Oh, goody. Just what she needed—dry busywork that was already done.

With a resigned sigh, she reached for the mouse just as the phone rang.

She picked up the receiver. "Hello?"

"Phoebe, it's Carson."

Her heart bounced. "Hey."

"Listen, Heidi heard Lily and I talking and found out about our conversation. She's pretty upset."

Phoebe closed her eyes. "Oh, no."

"Yeah. I tried explaining everything to her without going into too many details, but nothing helped." He drew in an audible breath. "Anyway, she pulled another disappearing trick and took off, and I'm stuck on these stupid crutches and can't go after her."

Alarm nipped at the edges of Phoebe's control. "Do you know where she went?" Phoebe asked.

"No idea."

Phoebe chewed on her lip, racking her brain. Heidi was upset…she wanted to be alone.…

Where had Phoebe herself gone when she was feeling like Heidi was? Bingo.

"I think I know where she went," she told Carson in a rush.

"Where?"

"It's just a hunch, but I think she went to my special spot on the beach."

"Can you go there and check?" he asked, obvious worry reflected in his tone.

"Sure thing."

"Thanks, Phoebe. If you find her, let me know."

"I will." She hung up, and then hustled out of her office to the store area. Tanya was just ringing up a sale, and the customer was digging for change at the bottom of a huge ugly purse.

Phoebe waited for a few seconds, mentally tapping a foot, then concerned impatience took over. "I'm leaving," she mouthed to Tanya, pointing toward the door.

Tanya nodded in acknowledgement.

Her heart galloping, Phoebe quickly headed out the front door, then turned left and jogged to the nearest beach access two blocks away. She scanned the steel-gray cloudy skies, noting the ever-present breeze was picking up and the temperature was dropping. The scent of the ocean hit her nose, and it smelled clean and crisp, tinged with moisture. Rain was on the way, maybe a summer storm.

As she hit the sand at a run, one thought pounded

through her with the force of a hammer. What would she do if something bad happened to Heidi?

She would need God's guidance for sure when she had her answer.

Carson wore a hole in the living-room carpet with his crutches, a sharp sense of helplessness hitting him from all sides. It figured he'd be laid up at a time like this, hobbled like a prisoner.

He stopped in front of the picture window, furrowing his brow. More clouds had rolled in, a steady rain now fell and a stiff wind slapped at the branches of the evergreens in the front yard. He hoped Phoebe found Heidi…and soon. No one should be out in this weather, much less an upset twelve-year-old wearing only a light sweatshirt.

With a snort of frustration, he turned away from the storm brewing at his doorstep. Thank goodness he had Phoebe and her hunch. He trusted her to bring Heidi back safe.

He trusted Phoebe…

Feeling suddenly boneless, he lowered himself to the couch, barely getting his crutches out from under his arms fast enough. He sat back as the truth wound its way around his consciousness like a soft ribbon: he trusted Phoebe implicitly, with the most important thing in his life—his daughter.

What did that tell him?

He loved Phoebe, that's what. Loved every single

thing about her—her kindness, her compassion, her beautiful smile.

Worry filtered through him. Without thought, his rigid hands came together in front of him, he bowed his head and a genuine prayer rose from his lips.

Please, Lord, help Phoebe find Heidi and bring them back to me.

His heart lifted, and somehow, he trusted God would answer his prayers and would watch over Heidi and Phoebe. A calming sense of peace spread through him, as warm and illuminating as the rays of the sun on a perfect summer day. With a deep sense of wonder, he realized Phoebe was right; there *was* peace in God. She had shown him the way to that comfort.

What an amazing, completely unforgettable woman.

One who obviously had used her faith to deal with her anger and forgive God enough to rely on her prayers to see her through difficult times, like now. She'd set a shining example for the path Carson needed to follow if he were ever going to be happy again.

He thought of Phoebe's lovely face, her innate kindness and comforting words of wisdom, and suddenly he didn't want to live in the shadows anymore. He wanted to live in the light of her love for the rest of his life.

A weight on his heart lifted, and he knew, in time, self-forgiveness would be his.

Then, like a rush of cold water, a shiver ran through

him. Phoebe wanted to say goodbye, wanted to run from him because of her fears.

He would be a fool to let her go. But baring his heart would be hard, knowing she had the power to crush his love with one little word.

Guess it was time for another chat with God. If anyone could help, He could.

Phoebe had taught him that.

Phoebe felt the first fat raindrops splash her face just as the Moonlight Cove Jetty came into clear view on her right. A gust of wind hit her, a stiff wall of air that had her jerking up the zipper on her hot-pink zip-up.

She shivered as she corralled her hair with one hand; it seemed as if the temperature had dropped dramatically in the past few minutes. Early summer on the Washington coast was capricious indeed.

Of course, it could be outright dread freezing her from the inside out. Where was Heidi? Had Phoebe's hunch been wrong?

Slogging through the drier and softer sand near the top of the beach, she cast her gaze left, away from the ocean, scanning the beach for signs of Heidi. Nothing.

Just as she found the rock that marked her favorite spot, a squiggle of movement to the right caught her eye. She snapped her head in that direction, searching the wave-roughened ocean surrounding the jetty.

After a few heart-pounding moments, she homed in on the source of movement, and her jaw dropped as alarm sizzled through her like a firecracker; there was a child squatted low on the very end of the long rock outcropping.

Heidi!

For the barest second, Phoebe stood immobile in shock, and in that space of time, a huge, storm-generated wave rose up and crashed around Heidi's feet and ankles, submerging the jetty, cutting off Heidi's escape.

"Help!" Heidi screamed, her cry of distress carrying to Phoebe on the wild wind.

Adrenaline shot through Phoebe, overriding her shock, and she instantly sprinted into action. "Heidi!" she shouted, raising her arms and waving as she ran toward the jetty. "Stay put!"

The jetty was made up of large, jagged rocks; one misstep or slip and Heidi could fall and hurt herself, or tumble into the churning ocean, which was splashing much higher than usual on the sloped sides of the jetty. Just last year, two teenagers on a school field trip had been swept out to sea off a jetty on the Oregon coast. Neither body had ever been found.

As chaotic, panic-fueled thoughts blasted Phoebe, she hit harder, wet sand, and the going was a bit easier. Even so, it seemed to take her an eternity to reach the inland end of the jetty where it met the beach.

She lurched to stop, her chest heaving, and sought Heidi with her gaze; luckily, she'd obeyed Phoebe and hadn't moved. "I'm coming to get you. Don't move," she yelled.

Grim-faced, Heidi nodded.

Phoebe gingerly started walking on the rocks toward Heidi, noting that many were slippery with algae, or was it moss? Whatever the case, the terrain was treacherous even in dry weather, and even more so with the wind and rain pelting everything in sight.

She had to keep her eyes on her rocky, jagged route instead of looking at Heidi, which didn't sit well with Phoebe; she wanted to know if she'd have to jump into the ocean to go after her. But, she told herself, if she never made it out to Heidi, Heidi's chances of safety were slimmer, so Phoebe doggedly kept her gaze focused down, carefully planning each step she took.

Thankfully, the waves seemed to have calmed down a bit, and the ocean wasn't slapping the sides of the jetty with as much force as it had been moments before. The final ten feet were the easiest, but by no means a piece of cake. The whole journey was harrowing.

The second Phoebe came within grabbing distance, Heidi glommed on to her with shaking hands. "I'm so glad you're here!" she said, her voice shrill, tinged with obvious terror. "I thought the waves were gonna knock me into the ocean."

With her heart in her throat, Phoebe adjusted her footing until it was steady, then looked directly at

Heidi. "I won't let you fall. But you have to do exactly what I say."

Heidi nodded, her damp hair hanging in her face. "Okay."

To her left, Phoebe saw a whitecap swell down low. Widening her eyes, she turned and simultaneously took a firmer hold on Heidi. With a sucking sound, the ocean rose up like a giant gray-green hand, a wall of water flecked with bits of seaweed coming at them full force.

"Duck!" she ordered, yelling as loud as she could, pulling Heidi down.

With a fear-tinted squeal, Heidi fell to the rocks with her. Then the giant wave crashed over Phoebe and Heidi, and a torrent of salt-scented sea water gushed over them, yanking and pulling, down, down, down.

With utter horror, Phoebe hung on to Heidi for dear life and stiffened her legs, sure she and Heidi were going to be swept out into the roiling, angry sea, never to be seen again.

Chapter Seventeen

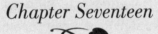

"Please protect us, God!"

The prayer lifted from Phoebe's lips, an automatic yet heartfelt plea. And then, like a perfect, wonderful gift, a distinct sense of tranquility came over her.

"I trust You, God, to watch over Heidi and me and keep us safe…"

As her mouth moved in prayer, and she connected with Him as surely as if He'd leaned down from His kingdom and she'd whispered right in His ear, an astonishing realization filtered through her brain: her faith in God was still there in her soul, burning bright and true and as strong as ever.

Astonished, she understood now that she had faith, always had, and she was ashamed she'd ever doubted her connection to God, that she'd let her anger blur their bond and mute her faith. Pure and cleansing, relief poured through her in a wave that was bigger and more profound than the one that had sprung from the stormy sea just moments ago.

As she crouched next to Heidi on the jetty and the wave crested, the water ran off her in a river of frigid liquid, soaking her to the bone. A shiver ran through Phoebe, salt water burned her eyes, and then the wave receded and drained off the rocks as quickly as it had come.

Breathless, her teeth chattering, she cast her gaze around to make sure there wasn't another wave on its way. Swells surrounded them, but no distinct waves had formed. Yet.

Seeing their chance for escape, she rose on shaky legs and pulled Heidi to her feet. "Come on, let's get out of here before another wave comes."

Pale-faced, Heidi nodded, then rose and grabbed Phoebe's hand and held on tight. Phoebe carefully navigated her way over the slick rocks as quickly as she could without falling while helping Heidi along, keeping an eye trained on the ocean in between steps to watch for any more threatening wave action.

The inland end of the jetty loomed far, far away, seemingly as easy to reach as the moon. But she kept moving, her eyes focused on safe ground, and as they progressed toward the shelter of dry land bit by bit, the seemingly insurmountable distance closed. Fifteen feet. Ten feet. Then five.

When Phoebe stepped onto the safety of the beach and felt solid ground beneath her feet, her eyes instantly filled with hot tears. Heidi followed her onto the sand, and with a sob, flung herself into Phoebe's arms, shaking with cold and, Phoebe was sure, shock mingled with immense relief.

They were safe.

Wiping drops of seawater from Heidi's face, Phoebe said, "Come on, honey. Let's get you home and warmed up."

"Are you mad at me for running off?" Heidi asked.

"I was worried, not mad," Phoebe replied, hugging Heidi again, so, so glad they weren't fish food. "So was your dad."

"I was just really upset that you'd left like my mom did."

Horror filled Phoebe. "Is that what you thought?"

Heidi nodded. "I know you called it quits with my dad."

"Yes, I did. But that doesn't mean you and I can't still be friends." She squeezed Heidi's shoulder. "I would never just desert you, sweetie. You'll always be part of my life."

"I know...but...I wanted you and my dad to be together," Heidi said in a very tiny voice. "And...I really was hoping you might be my mom."

Phoebe's chest tightened and her eyes burned. "That's the best thing anybody has ever said to me."

"But?"

She took Heidi's hand and started walking. "But... it's complicated, and grown-up relationships are tricky." And scary. And took more courage than Phoebe had.

"They don't seem tricky to me."

Phoebe frowned. "Really? Why is that?"

"Because if you love someone, then what else matters?"

Heidi's statement landed like a bomb inside of Phoebe.

Before Phoebe could choke out a response, Heidi tightened her grip on her hand. "Thank you for saving my life," she said, her voice cracking as a shudder ran through her.

"I didn't save you. God did," Phoebe replied.

"You think?" Heidi asked, her nose scrunched.

"Definitely. I asked Him to protect us, and He did."

Heidi shivered and pressed closer to Phoebe's side. "I didn't realize going out on the jetty was that dangerous."

Dangerous. The word echoed in Phoebe's head. "Lots of things are dangerous, even if they don't look it," Phoebe said, actually *hearing* her words as she spoke, beginning to understand their true meaning. "Even things that seem safe."

"Yeah, I guess."

Phoebe barely registered Heidi's reply over the loud voice screaming in her head, saying *Look at me! Listen!*

So she did look and listen for a split second. And in that tiny yet important beat of time, an astonishing realization whacked her, hard.

Peril was all around, no matter who you were or what you did. Whether you were a twelve-year-old girl or an ice-cream-store owner or a cop. And if she lived her life and made her choices according to what *might* happen, if she feared that danger would take away her security by striking down the people she loved, she'd be frozen in place forever, without true happiness.

And she desperately wanted to be happy. Not just run-of-the-mill, so-so happy. But intense, wonderful, joyous, yell-out-in-bliss happy.

And she finally knew how to achieve that.

She had to lay her heart bare and tell Carson she loved him. And if he returned her feelings, love would provide all the security she'd ever need.

But…what if he wasn't willing to forgive her for already saying goodbye?

Heidi's wise words came back to her. *If you love someone, then what else matters?*

Nothing. Nothing else mattered but her love for Carson, not even Phoebe's own worries about whether or not Carson would forgive her. She saw now that she had to follow her heart and take the leap.

His good leg trembling, but unable to sit still, Carson stood looking out the front window, his eyes trained on the rain-slicked street, as if Phoebe and Heidi would simply materialize there, conjured up by his thoughts, and end his worry.

He had the phone clenched in his hand to call 911 if he didn't hear from Phoebe in the next few minutes; he was almost at the end of his rope.

Just as the rope pulled taut and he was ready to lift the phone to his ear, it rang.

He quickly pressed the talk button. "Yes?" he barked.

"I found her," Phoebe said. "She's fine."

Relief spread through him in a warm, soothing wave. "Oh, thank God." For the first time in his life, he really meant that statement.

"I'm going to drive her over to your house. We'll be there soon."

"Okay."

He hung up, and his spine sagged in release. His two girls were safe. Crisis averted. And that meant he'd been given an opportunity to tell Heidi what she needed to hear. What a wonderful gift, one he wasn't about to squander. Nothing was more important than making sure Heidi knew he'd always be there for her.

And what about him and Phoebe? Was it time for the next chapter in his life to begin? And if so, would Phoebe be there when he turned the page?

With that important question still on his mind, he waited on the porch. Ten minutes later, Phoebe's compact car pulled up into the driveway.

He gingerly made his way down the stairs on his crutches, thankful the rain had dwindled to a light mist for the time being.

Heidi popped out of the car and ran up the cement walkway, her damp hair flying behind her. "Daddy!" she cried, flinging herself into his arms.

He managed to keep his balance and embrace her, tight, even holding on to his crutches somehow. More relief poured through him as he pressed a kiss to the top of her head; he was so glad to have his baby home safe. On the periphery of his senses, he noticed her clothes were soaking wet.

He pulled back, and Phoebe came around the car. She, too, was soaked, and paler than he'd ever seen her, her eyes filling up her face like huge sapphires.

His heart twisted at the sight of her, and, wordlessly, he lifted an arm. She stepped into his embrace and snuggled close, and he pulled her near, right up against him, right where she belonged.

Something intangible melted inside of him, and somehow he knew that nothing else would ever be the same if he lost this wonderful woman.

The three of them stood there for a few quiet moments, and then he leaned back and said, "What happened?"

"I got trapped out on the rock thing." Heidi smoothed her wet hair behind her ear. "I was really scared."

He frowned. "Rock thing?"

"The beach jetty," Phoebe said.

"Phoebe saved my life," Heidi announced. "The waves were big and were crashing around me, so she came out onto the jetty to get me. Another wave got us, but we held on and then made it off the jetty."

He looked at Phoebe. "Was it really that bad?"

"Dad!" Heidi said.

"Just making sure," he replied, adjusting his crutches underneath him.

"The waves were bigger than normal, and the rocks were slick, so yes, it was bad," Phoebe told him.

"See?" Heidi lifted her chin. "I told you."

Carson froze, the true enormity of the situation hitting him full force; someone could have been hurt, or worse. Oh, man. What would he have done if his worst nightmare had come to life and something had happened to Phoebe or Heidi? The question didn't even bear answering.

But the dicey query *did* show him what he had to do. Right now. Before the amazing woman who'd saved his daughter got it in her head that he was going to let her walk out of his life without a battle of epic proportions.

"Let's go inside and get you two into some dry clothes," he suggested.

"Good idea," Phoebe said, rubbing her upper arms. "I'm freezing."

Well, at least she was willing to stay awhile. A good sign? Or was she just being practical, wanting to get warm?

His heart racing, he hobbled his way inside behind Heidi and Phoebe just as more raindrops began falling. Looked as though the storm wasn't over.

When they reached the foyer, Heidi hit the stairs. "I'll get you something to wear," she said to Phoebe.

Phoebe went to follow her upstairs. "I'll come help you."

Carson held up a hand. "Heidi?"

Heidi swung around. "Yeah?"

"Come here."

She walked down a few stairs and stopped in front of him, her blue eyes bright against her pale skin.

"I'm bad at sharing my feelings, and I know I haven't been very good about making you feel secure." He put his arms around her and drew her close once more; she smelled like seawater and ocean breeze. He hesitated as words clogged his throat. Instinctually, he looked over Heidi's damp head at Phoebe.

With a gentle smile, Phoebe nodded encouragingly, as if to say, *go on, you're doing great.*

He swallowed, wanting to do the right thing—for Heidi and Phoebe. And himself, too, because if Heidi was healthy and happy, so was he. "I want you to know that I love you, and I will never, ever leave you, no matter what."

Heidi sagged against him. "I know, Dad, but thanks for telling me."

An immense sense of relief washed over him. "We need to keep talking to each other, all right? You tell me when you're upset, and we'll work it out. You don't run off, ever again. You hear me?"

"Okay," she mumbled into his chest. "After today, I know better."

"You told me that the last time this happened." He put his hand under her chin and forced her to look at him. "I'm going to need to ground you this time, Heidi, so I'm sure you realize how important it is not to run away every time you get upset."

She let out a large breath, then nodded. "Okay, whatever you say."

He pulled back, his hands firm on her shoulders. "I want a promise you're never going to pull this stunt again, or you're going to give me a heart attack to go along with my broken ankle, and that'll be way more than I can handle."

She made an X over her chest. "Cross my heart."

"Good deal." He turned her around and gave her a gentle push toward the stairs. "Now go get changed."

"Aye-aye, Captain Winters," she said on a giggle as she dodged Phoebe and went upstairs, taking the steps two at a time.

Phoebe followed, but he called out, "Hold on a sec, Phoebe." His work wasn't done. Not by a long shot. He and Heidi were good. Now it was time to make things right with Phoebe.

Wide-eyed, Phoebe spun around just as her foot hit the third stair. Heidi stopped at the top of the landing. Two blue gazes locked on him.

"As soon as you get changed, we need to talk," he said to Phoebe quietly.

She silently nodded.

Heidi came back down a few stairs. "What's going on?"

"You take Phoebe up and get changed," he said, pointing upstairs with his right crutch. "And then Phoebe and I need to have a private conversation."

"Ooh. Private." Heidi wagged her brows. "Sounds good."

He gave her a poker face.

With a snort, she crooked a hand. "Come on, Phoebe. I'll loan you something of mine."

Without a word, Phoebe followed her upstairs.

And Carson waited, his stomach churning, for her to come back down. And make or break his happiness.

After what seemed an interminable wait, but was really only ten minutes, Phoebe returned dressed in a too-small pair of gray sweatpants, a white T-shirt with some swoop-haired teenybopper boy band on the front and a pair of white athletic socks. Her damp hair hung loose around her shoulders, starting to curl wildly around her face.

"Pretty, I know," she said, pirouetting in front of him.

He cocked a brow. "Actually, you look adorable."

"Thanks. I think," she said, giving him a sideways glance.

Silence.

Finally, she raised her chin. "So, let's talk. I have something to say, too."

Anxiety wove sharp tentacles through him. "Okay. Let's go into the living room and sit down." Not that he'd ever admit it, but his ankle was starting to throb relentlessly. Too much standing and worrying.

She spun on her heel and marched into the room. He followed, almost knocking her over with one crutch when she stopped abruptly and he plowed into her.

"Sorry," she said in unison with him.

Once they'd both righted themselves, he said, "You go first," at the exact time she said, "You go first."

He looked at the floor. "Apparently we're on the same page." Unless she was on the I'm-going-to-dump-you-all-over-again page. And then they definitely weren't on the same page, or even reading the same book. Just let her try and run away.

She remained silent.

"Why don't we just say what we have to say together," he offered. "Then no one is put on the spot."

She inclined her head to the side. "Fair enough."

"On three, all right?"

"Okeydoke."

Taking a deep breath, he said, "One. Two. Three."

"I love you," he said.

"I love you," she said at the exact same time.

He stared at her, hanging on to her clear blue gaze, his breathing shallow and hitched. His heart took a tentative little hop of joy. "Did you just happen to say you loved me?" he asked, his voice husky.

A charming blush spread across her cheeks. "I did."

His breathing snagged. "What made you change your mind?"

"The ocean and the jetty," she said with a little shrug. "And your remarkably smart daughter."

"Huh?"

She grinned and stepped closer, and even though she'd been doused in seawater, her fresh clean scent reached out and tickled his nose. "After we reached land, Heidi said she didn't know the ocean and the jetty could be so dangerous. And that made me realize that danger is everywhere, for you, me and everybody. Life happens. That, in turn, helped me to see that letting my fears hold me away from loving you wasn't what was going to make me happy."

"So, how did Heidi help?"

"Oh, just with a few profound words along the lines of, 'if you love someone then nothing else matters.'"

His throat tightened. "So now that the ocean and my twelve-year-old daughter have had their say, what *is* going to make you happy?" he asked, caressing her smooth-as-silk cheek.

"You are," she said, simply. Yet he'd never heard more profound, or welcome, words.

A response stuck in his throat as joy ricocheted through his heart.

"And by the way," she said, grinning up at him in an adorable way that he would never get tired of, "You were right when you said I was using your job as an excuse to keep from taking a risk."

"I'm a genius," he replied, shifting his weight to his good leg and bending down to rest his forehead against hers. "And that's why I'm never letting you go."

"Then I guess we love each other, don't we?" She came to within an inch of his lips.

"Guess we do." He let his crutches fall to the floor and gathered her close, erasing the tiny bit of space between them.

And he sealed the whole deal with a kiss.

A long time later, he came up for air, smoothing her damp hair back with his hand. "Glad we have that all cleared up."

Eyes shining with happiness looked up at him. "You can say that again."

He bent down and kissed his way to her ear. "I want you to be in my life forever," he whispered, stating his deepest wish, no holds barred.

Her arms came around him and she pressed herself close. "As a family, you, me and Heidi?"

"Of course," he said, burying his nose in her neck. "One big happy family."

"Hey, you two."

He broke away and spun around at the same time Phoebe did.

Heidi, dressed in fuzzy pink sweats, stood in the living room doorway, grinning so big he was sure her face was going to crack. "What's going on here?"

"You want to break the happy news?" Phoebe said, her mouth crooked into a beautiful, happy smile he would never get tired of seeing.

He nodded. "I do." Turning, he looked at Heidi, his mouth turned up so far it almost hurt. Almost. "We're in love."

With a whoop of joy, Heidi launched herself at them. As he stood on one foot, with Phoebe's quick action helping out, he caught half of Heidi while Phoebe caught the other half. Were they good partners, or what?

And then he had both of his girls in his arms, and

he knew without a doubt that Phoebe had given him the one thing he wanted most in the world—peace.

Coupled with love, how could they go wrong?

Epilogue

"I now pronounce you husband and wife," Pastor Goodrich announced, his booming voice filling the sanctuary. "You may kiss the bride."

From her position on the altar next to Molly, feeling nothing like an eggplant or purple dinosaur in her bridesmaid dress, Phoebe looked on as her beaming best friend and Grant kissed before all of their family and friends.

When the ecstatic bride and groom pulled apart from their long kiss, a warm cheer went up, and Molly looked right at Phoebe. Molly quirked a brow and gave a brief tilt of her head, as if to say, *are you going to be next?*

Phoebe shrugged, holding her hopes close, not wanting to assume too much. Yet. But deep down, she had dreams for a wedding of her own in the near future, with the most perfect man on the planet standing at the altar with her, saying their vows before God.

That thought automatically had her eyes seeking

out Carson and Heidi sitting in the second row of the church.

Carson, looking more handsome than ever in a dark blue suit, snow-white dress shirt and navy blue patterned tie, winked and threw her a small yet private smile that made Phoebe's breath catch. Heidi, quite the young lady with her hair pulled up, wore a pretty pink frock Phoebe had helped her pick out. Heidi waved, grinning brightly.

Phoebe's heart just about collapsed in pure happiness. How had she ever thought letting the sheriff and his daughter into her heart would be a bad thing?

The past month had been a whirlwind of helping with Molly's wedding preparations sprinkled with lots of time spent with Carson and Heidi. Phoebe felt as if they were a family already, and the thought of making the connection permanent thrilled her.

She had a suspicion Carson felt the same way, given how close they'd become in the past few weeks, since that day they'd both realized they belonged together.

The wedding march rang out from the church organ, and Molly and Grant, holding hands, stepped off the altar and headed up the center aisle of the church. Phoebe and the rest of the wedding party filed out behind them.

As she approached Carson and Heidi, Phoebe mouthed to Heidi, "You look beautiful!"

Heidi mouthed back, "You, too!"

Phoebe paused for a brief moment as she waited to continue up the aisle, clutching her bouquet in her hands, and looked at the man she loved. His gaze held hers, warm and filled with a tenderness that never failed to make her melt.

He pressed a hand to his heart, then gestured to her, as if he were giving her all of the love he held inside of him.

With her own mushy heart bursting to overflowing, she mirrored the gesture, holding his gaze, knowing that nothing would ever pull her from his side.

The wedding party continued on up the aisle. Phoebe followed, feeling as if she were walking on air as she sent her thanks up to God for helping her find such a perfect love, for helping her to believe that second chances were possible, even for her.

And then, with her head held high and her heart finally, blissfully complete, Phoebe stepped from the flower-bedecked sanctuary into the sunlit church foyer, ready to start her new life with an amazing man and his wonderful daughter by her side. As a family.

Forever.

* * * * *

Dear Reader,

Welcome back to Moonlight Cove! I'm so excited to be writing more books about my favorite beach town, and equally excited that I have readers like you who join me as two stubborn people fall in love when they least expect it. I hope you enjoy reading about Phoebe and Carson's rocky road to true love and that their story touches your heart and reminds you that with a little faith, second chances are always possible.

Some of the themes in this book are based on my own experiences. Who hasn't experienced grief over losing a loved one? This thought led me to write a story in which the hero and heroine are brought together by shared feelings of loss and sadness, only to discover that life does get better after a devastating loss, and that love and faith help heal wounds wrought by grief.

I truly enjoy hearing from readers, so please feel free to contact me either through Love Inspired, or at www.lissamanley.com.

Blessings,
Lissa

Questions for Discussion

1. Carson insisted on some kind of consequence for Heidi's shoplifting. Was he too harsh? Not harsh enough? Why or why not? What other consequences could he have imposed? In your opinion, did his occupation as a cop dictate his reaction? Or did his role as a father have more influence?

2. Phoebe didn't believe in second chances, and truly believed she would only have one true love. How was this belief flawed? Or not?

3. Was Mrs. Philpot responsible for Heidi's sneaking out of the house? If so, how could she have handled the situation differently? Was she a bad caretaker, or was Heidi just sneaky enough to slip by anyone?

4. Phoebe went to grief counseling to make her mother happy. Was this a wrongheaded way to go about handling her grief? What else could she have done to deal with the loss of her fiancé?

5. Carson blamed himself for his son's death. Discuss whether you agree with his self-blame or not, and why. Did he have control over his guilt, or not? How would you have reacted in this situation?

6. Phoebe unwittingly broke Carson's confidence by telling Heidi she knew about her brother's death. Were her actions justified given the situation? How could she have handled the discussion with Heidi differently while still letting Heidi know she empathized with her?

7. Was it realistic of Carson to expect to keep CJ's death a secret? Was he simply trying to sweep the tragedy under the rug, or were his actions understandable given the situation and his character? Discuss.

8. Carson called Phoebe on not depending on the faith she touted as being so helpful in dealing with grief, turning her advice back on her. Discuss why you think Phoebe had a harder time helping herself than helping Carson. Is it harder for most people to see the solutions to their own problems? Why or why not?

9. Carson felt asking for help was a sign of weakness. Why did he feel this way? Was this reaction realistic? Talk about how you feel when you have to ask for help.

10. Discuss why you think Carson had a difficult time opening up to Phoebe. Was this difficulty justified, or not? Why? How has this kind of reaction affected your life?

11. Discuss how CJ was killed, and whether or no Carson should have left him alone to take dow the perp. Also discuss whether his role of Da should have overridden his role as cop, or vic versa, and why.

12. Did Carson deserve the guilt he carried over CJ' death? Depending on your answer, how should h have decided how much guilt he deserved? Wher should he have drawn the line? Is there a line' Does it change as time passes? Discuss.

13. Carson's accident on the job reminded Phoeb how she felt when her fiancé died, and soon after she told Carson that she couldn't let herself lov him for fear of losing him one way or another Discuss whether her thinking was skewed, an how she could have handled this situation differ ently. Were her actions justified, given her char acter and what she'd been through?

14. Phoebe realized the world was full of danger whe she rescued Heidi from the jetty, which resulte in a change in the way she viewed loving Carson Discuss why or why not this epiphany was be lievable, and whether she would have ultimatel admitted she loved Carson if she hadn't had th experience on the jetty.

5. Heidi's way of handling conflict was to run away. Discuss whether this was a valid way to operate, and how her gut reactions to stress might change as she gets older.

SUSPENSE

RIVETING INSPIRATIONAL ROMANCE

Watch for our series of edge-
of-your-seat suspense novels.
These contemporary tales
of intrigue and romance
feature Christian characters
facing challenges to their faith...
and their lives!

AVAILABLE IN REGULAR
& LARGER-PRINT FORMATS

For exciting stories that reflect traditional values,
visit:
www.ReaderService.com